Tourist Trap

Tourist Trap

by TED STRATTON

G. P. Putnam's Sons
New York

COPYRIGHT © 1975 BY TED STRATTON

*All rights reserved. This book, or parts thereof, must not
be reproduced in any form without permission.
Published simultaneously in Canada
by Longman Canada Limited, Toronto.*

SBN: 399-11608-7

Library of Congress Catalog
Card Number: 75-21827

PRINTED IN THE UNITED STATES OF AMERICA

1

ON THURSDAY morning September 6, Captain Fred Raber of the Fair Hills Police Department swung an unmarked car into Mercer Street and parked adjacent to the extension of the Municipal Building. Sized like a welterweight, he had short black hair, blue eyes, and a tanned face with such a youthful expression that it subtracted three or four years from his actual age, thirty-four. He wore a short-sleeved white shirt, a blue tie clipped with a silver bar, gray trousers, and Oxfords. Only a snub-nosed .357 Magnum in a belt holster identified him as a police officer.

He climbed the stairs to the second floor and arrived inside headquarters. Ahead stood a gate marked NO ADMITTANCE, an aisle behind an illuminated, traditionally high desk, a door at the aisle's end into an extensive rear area and, on the left, a bank of filing cabinets under windows masked by venetian blinds.

Lieutenant Dick Sprague, a stocky veteran ten years older than Raber, offered an affable, "Good morning. You were in and gone before I came on tour," he said.

"A couple of errands," Raber said. "Mail arrive?"

"Yes, and checked. Routine, except a personal letter for you from our vacationing chief. On your desk, captain."

"Thanks."

Raber rounded the desk and paused to smile at probationary officer Sande Nosse, a slim, married blonde, also on duty. She wore a white shirtwaist with a blue patch lettered FHPD, a blue skirt, blue nylons, and blue pumps.

"How's the training program going?" Raber asked.

"Interestingly," she answered. "I know it's illegal for nosies and criminals to monitor our shortwave, but since they do it anyway I have to learn all our doubletalk. Care to test me, captain?"

"A Hank Aaron order."

"Sirens blasting, move in hard and fast."

"How's Greta Garbo today?"

"Emergency, *phone* HQ within forty seconds."

"Uncode BDG-6."

"Fair Hills divided into four zones," Nosse ticked off. "First letter identifies zone, next two streets, six no siren." She glanced at an instruction chart prominent alongside the microphone. "Uncoded, squad car's pinpoint target, southeast quadrant, corner Glen and Maple. I already know the squad car's initial position, calculate its arrival time at the pinpoint, then feed exact address to the officer, say 228 Glen, plus reason. Make this one suspicious car, two men. Captain, the doubletalk works?"

Raber prompted: "Dick?"

"May twenty-second, current," Sprague said, the possessor of a remarkable memory. "Phone call, housewife, nine twenty A.M. Three strangers, car, behind a neighbor's house. To nearest squad car, shot a Greta Garbo. Second car, three miles distant, zone code. First officer phoned promptly, received details. We waited, ticking off the time, then ordered a Hank Aaron. We heard two sirens come on, then the screech of brakes and slam of car doors. Silence, Nosse, two officers going in with drawn .38's. They caught one robber still monitoring our shortwave in their car, one carrying out a portable TV, and halted three with a warning shot."

"That 'we' meant the lieutenant alone at the mike and *we* expect you to become as competent as he," Raber said as he entered his small office that had been partitioned from the rear area when he had been appointed a captain in June.

Standing at the rear of the desk, he switched on a low lamp and opened a letter. It seemed the chief and Mrs. Hocking enjoyed Wildwood Crest, the magnificent beach, the seafood, the perfect weather, and the lack of daily irritation, the last-mentioned to be reencountered at eight A.M., Monday, September 10. P.S. "Freddy, I know the training program for the three female officers has been in top gear while I've been gone—congrats." Raber dropped the letter into a drawer and switched off the light.

In June Fair Hills' borough council had provided additional funds to hire three new police officers to meet the expanding needs of a population of 17,000. Even today, rumors persisted in the department as to why three women had been added to an all-male force.

1. To outwit a newly organized Women's Lib group.

2. Previously, coffee brewed in the back area and served in cracked mugs had been so rank that all males were cranky. Now, females brewed excellent coffee served in real china cups, plus saucers, and the consumption of Alka-Seltzer had dropped to nil.

3. The chief's favorite TV program was *Adam 12*. The department's wag, Sergeant Parisi joked: "Secretly the chief's in love with that anonymous female dispatcher and her low-keyed voice. So we get ourselves three female dispatchers so the chief can loll in his office and drool. All dolls, too."

In retrospect Raber smiled because there had been other cogent reasons for the appointment of the women.

He and the chief had reasoned it was a waste of trained, experienced personnel to station lieutenants and sergeants at the desk, in the traditional manner, since the job was essentially clerical and said personnel belonged on the firing line. Also, the bane of every officer's life was the preparation of endless reports, pecked out on typewriters or written laboriously in longhand. When the borough advertised for recruits, all applicants were required to be proficient in stenography. Twenty-two women and three men had taken the written Civil Service exams administered by the State Police. Sanda Nosse, Rose Scafide, and Grace Gladwyn, the last a black, scored the highest marks and also passed the steno tests. For three months they had handled all typing chores including transcribing officers' reports from tape recorders. Today it was a pleasure to read typed logs, typed reports, and—

At the front desk a man announced: "I'm Harry Shellenbach. Just drove up Route Seventeen from Newark and I have a problem."

"Lieutenant Sprague, sir. What's your problem?"

"I'm lost in your town."

Shellenbach leaned against the desk and Raber studied him. He was in his late thirties, wore a sports jacket, an open-necked yellow shirt, tan trousers, and brown loafers.

"Tell me about it," Sprague suggested.

"Well, I had this map and located the turn off Route Seventeen into your Broad Street. I parked for a final check of the map because the instructions were complicated. Damned if I hadn't mislaid the map! I continued slowly along Broad, spotted a big building on the right and a corner sign, POLICE HEADQUARTERS. So, here I am, lieutenant."

"Where you headed, Mr. Shellenbach?"

"Twin Springs Trout Club for a week's vacation."

"Return to Broad and continue west. Cross the Erie Railroad. At the second street, Harristown Road, turn right, half mile to a T-intersection with—"

Shellenbach interrupted. "I remember, with Haymow Road!"

"Haycock," Sprague corrected. "Left turn, one mile. Twin Springs is on the left, you can't miss the sign. You'll enjoy the finest private trout fishing in the East, sir."

"So friends advised. And I expect to enjoy the hospitality of the owners, Mr. and Mrs. Barrington."

"The Barringtons sold out on April first."

"Hmmm, that's a surprise. Who are the new owners?"

"Empire Export and Import Company."

"My God, that sounds cold! What's this new outfit like?"

"Well, five male employees. I understand the club is still tops, terrific fishing and accommodations."

"Yes, but—"

Shellenbach hesitated.

"This is a letdown after all my friends told me about the Barringtons. Can you fill me in about the company, the employees?"

4

Raber wrote a terse message on a memo pad, tore off the sheet, and strolled into the main room.

He said, "I overheard your little problem, Mr. Shellenbach." The man faced him. "Look, Broad Street intersects us east-west. Erie Railroad north-south. That divides our burg into four sections, see? Keep remembering Twin Springs is northeast an' you got it."

"Simple," Shellenbach commented blandly.

Raber added, "Pardon us a tick-tock," and rounded the desk to show Sprague the memo, which read: *Hold him for two minutes.*

"Where do I find the answer?" Raber asked.

"Back area, captain. Try the file under Boyce."

Raber pushed through a door solid, except for the louvered bottom. The large area contained an interrogation room, the protrusion of his office, a darkroom, work desks, individual lockers for all officers, a shower stall, a lavatory, sink, refrigerator, typewriters and tape recorders, and lab equipment.

Roy Boyce, detective second-grade, sat at a desk peering into a microscope. He glanced up, saw Raber place a finger to his lips, and nodded in understanding. He was a young, blue-eyed blonde with such a cherubic facial expression that Parisi had called him "Angel-face," and the nickname had become permanent.

"Stranger at the desk with a fuzzy story," Raber detailed softly. "Where's the car parked?"

"Across the street," Boyce whispered.

"Make like a citizen," Raber ordered, and Boyce rose and stripped off the shield on his shirt. "This joker says he's headed for a week's fishing at Twin Springs. I want a full make on the smart aleck."

Alongside his shield atop the desk, Boyce laid a holstered Magnum, handcuffs, and a summons book.

"How long do I have?"

"A minute."

Boyce hurried to the rear of the room and disappeared. At a side window, Raber parted a venetian blind. Seconds later,

Boyce trotted across Mercer Street, opened the door of a new Ford, and waved a hand. Raber strolled into headquarters.

"Your best bet for information on the new owners," Sprague was saying, "is the Barringtons. They live in a white farmhouse two hundred yards beyond the club entrance. You can't miss that, Mr. Shellenbach. It's on the opposite side of Haycock Road."

"Good idea," Shellenbach acknowledged. "When I'm settled in a lodge I'll pay them a visit."

"You all set, fellow?" Raber asked.

"Of course."

"Just say the word, Mr. Shellenbark. I'll yank in a squad car, give you a police escort right out to Twin Springs."

"Thanks, but not at all necessary."

Striding around the desk, Shellenbach entered the stairwell and disappeared. Below, a door closed.

"Read him," Raber ordered.

"Page one, open book," Sprague said. "A smart aleck from the city who downgraded the intelligence of the local police. Used a flimsy excuse to drop in and try to pump us. Probably a private detective at work on a local case, Twin Springs. My guess, he's already been out there or is in residence. You put Roy on him?"

"Shellenbach has a police escort from the rear."

"Please, just one moment!" Nosse exclaimed, and both officers turned to face her. "I heard everything that nice man said! Lost in a strange town, stopped here for directions, and now he wears a tail!"

"Ah, but he could have obtained directions to Twin Springs from anybody on Broad Street," Raber suggested. "Dick?"

"Nosse, what a stranger says and what's in his mind are often at variance. Twin Springs' weekly rates are two hundred fifty dollars. Wealthy guests arrive in cars from all over the East. Management supplies a map which smart aleck had. A child could remember those directions and follow them to Twin Springs from Route Seventeen with no trouble. But that guy had to insert Haymow for Haycock

Road. Nosse, every day you come to work you drive past that sign at the corner of Broad. What does it say?"

She thought a moment, then: " 'Municipal Building, Borough of Fair Hills. Elevation eight hundred feet. Population seventeen thousand.' The sign to police headquarters is a block farther in, at Mercer."

"Correct. So your nice man lied to us. How do I know he's a private working a local case? Because any other type of operative would *first* produce his credentials, cue us with as much as we needed to know to understand his problem, and then ask for our cooperation. Not this cutie. He even pretended not to know Twin Springs had changed management on April first."

Sprague returned to Raber.

"Captain, I won't say Shellenbach was scared, but I was closer to him than you, and he was sweating. I think he bumped into something out at Twin Springs that he didn't expect or something too damned big for him to handle."

"Good analysis," Raber said.

"But I don't understand it all!" Nosse exclaimed. "Admitted he tried to pump us—and lied. Do we tail every stranger who enters here?"

"Officer," Raber said, "don't you forget for one second that this eighty square miles of territory, pretty wild in spots, and its seventeen thousand residents, are our prime responsibility for twenty-four hours a day."

Nosse noticed a slight change in Raber, a coldness in his blue eyes.

"Nobody runs around our territory doing whatever he pleases, poking his nose into corners and barging in here to treat us like dummies. Maybe I put Boyce on Shellenbach because the man bruised my ego. Maybe it was only a defense mechanism, too many people try to belittle our legal authority. Or I just wanted to ensure that a police officer is always— you bet, *always*—alert on his mental toes or he should turn in his badge."

"Nosse," Sprague drawled, "the captain suggests a good officer should be curious about everything he observes and hears. No matter how innocuous or irrelevant something seems, a good officer runs it through his mind, then stores it up, just in case."

"This spring," Raber snapped, "I was away on a police seminar. We had a spot of trouble at Twin Springs. I missed something important?"

"Relax, you're a very busy officer," Sprague soothed. "Also, for the benefit of Nosse, Twin Springs is the second-biggest taxpayer in the borough and always rated our special service. Poachers bothered them, locals after some of those big trout for free. So, four or five times a week, a squad car circled the pond road, always at different hours. We nabbed three, four poachers, shooed others off, and the word got around to lay off. The Barringtons appreciated our work. On April eleventh, around six fifteen A.M., Bill Mader ran a spot check. He circled quietly, then stopped to use binoculars. When he passed the office in the farmhouse on his way out their new superintendent, Joe Arragon, stopped him. Arragon's a big man, asked Mader what the hell he was doing on private property. Mader explained the procedure. Arragon told Mader never to come back, the same for other squad cars. Okay. I came on tour at eight and read Mader's report. I made a special note and placed it on the chief's desk. He drove out there in a squad car, met Arragon and a man in his mid-fifties, name of Gene Palan, handles the office. The chief told them word of mouth was not sufficient to stop the routine patrols, and to put the request in writing. That letter is in the files, captain. You ever see it?"

"No."

Sprague turned to the bank of files, pulled out a drawer, extracted a letter from a folder, and handed it to Raber. The communication was written in neat longhand on stationery with the heading Twin Springs Trout Club, Fair Hills, New Jersey, 10045, dated April 11.

> TO CHIEF LAIRD HOCKING:
> We appreciate the fact one of your squad cars circled our pond on a routine patrol at 6:20 A.M. today. However, we consider such patrols absolute-

ly unnecessary. The presence of police cars on our private property, other than during some unforeseen or totally unexpected emergency, introduces disturbing notes into the bucolic atmosphere which it is our intention to preserve at all times. This letter relieves your department of any necessity to patrol the private property, at any time, of Twin Springs Trout Club. If there should arise an incident within your authority, we shall telephone your department for assistance.

Cordially, and signed,
JOE ARRAGON, superintendant.

Raber returned the letter.

"That's the status quo since April eleventh," Sprague added. "Not one squad car has disturbed their bucolic atmosphere."

"Most large property owners," Raber observed, "feel they never receive sufficient police protection. How do you spell your new title?"

"L-i-e-u-t-e-n-a-n-t."

"French word, unusual spelling. Why learn to spell it?"

"Fred, French or Polish or Yiddish word, I'd feel uncomfortable if I couldn't spell my title correctly."

"Friend Arragon misspelled *his* title," Raber murmured. "Added in *his* handwriting after *his* signature." Raber addressed Nosse. "Phone Mrs. Morrison, Tax Office. I arrive there in five minutes. Ask her please to have the plat maps of Twin Springs available."

Nosse busied herself on the interbuilding phone system.

"Dick, this Palan wrote the letter and he handles the office. Why didn't he type the letter? Can't he type? If not, he handles all club correspondence in longhand?"

"Maybe he hunts and pecks on a machine," Sprague suggested.

"Possibly. I read him as a highly educated man. Ummm, the Barringtons sold everything to Empire?"

"Except for heirlooms."

"Including their jeep?"

"The jeep still wears the club name on both sides. Saw it parked in town last week."

"Thanks. The jeep item might come in handy."

"Captain, you're expected at the tax office," Nosse said.

As Raber pushed through the door into the main building, he heard Nosse ask, "Why did the captain twice mispronounce Mr. Shellenbach's name?"

Raber paused in the corridor, the door ajar.

"Sande," Sprague approved, "your ears are becoming trained. Just a stratagem to further convince that smart aleck we are stupid. If he continues to believe he has the superior brain, we obtain a greater advantage that some day might—"

Raber let the door swing shut.

2

COLONIAL IN design, the main Municipal Building had been constructed during the Great Depression with federal funds and the new wing added in 1962 to face Mercer Street so the complex formed a capital *L*. Opposite police headquarters lay a huge room for community affairs, positioned above the police garage and the area housing the rigs of the volunteer fire department.

Raber followed a corridor, turned right, and entered the main building. Windows abutted the main street and to his left were departmental offices. He entered the Tax Office where Mrs. Morrison, an attractive widow, presided in an anteroom.

"Good morning, captain," she said pleasantly. "Is something big brewing at Twin Springs that requires police attention?"

In this hive, he knew he had to squelch a gossip item before it burgeoned out of proportion, so he explained casually, "I haven't been out there for years and decided I should refresh my mind on the many improvements."

"The plat maps are ready on a table in Mr. Larrimore's office. Just call me if there is a question."

"Is the boss available?"

"He's due back any minute."

In a spacious office stood a cluttered desk, a number of chairs, and a long table where plat maps were arranged to form a solid pattern held in place by thumbtacks. Raber noted that the present area of Twin Springs in the borough comprised 80.7 acres and began to recall some of its history.

In the 1890's, millionaire Otto Koenig, a New York City banker, assembled a huge estate, largely in adjoining Cumberland Township and extending across the Ramapo River to a mountainous ridge called The Rampart. He erected a mansion near the river and began the life of a country squire. Later, in a valley in Fair Hills where two tremendous springs originated, Koenig built a dam with lodges at either end and four more lodges in the woods. Guests fished the stocked pond and hunted the adjoining land for deer and stocked pheasants and other upland game. When Koenig died after World War I, heirs boarded up the mansion and sold off the estate in smaller parcels. The present 80.7 acres, plus twenty acres across Haycock Road in Cumberland Township, were purchased by a prosperous farmer, Jonas Lane. He had one child, a daughter, who married John Barrington, a sportsman who saw possibilities in the lovely pond. When the daughter inherited the property, Barrington restocked the pond with trout, advertised, and lured fishermen to the area. As business prospered, he added six more lodges.

Raber studied the map and its inked notations.

A large farmhouse abutted Haycock Road. A lane arced around the farmhouse, passed an ample barn with an upstairs apartment, and then circled the pond. Next to the barn were breeding pools for trout plus a one-story stable that ran parallel to the rear of the farmhouse. At the dam's north end, the first guest lodge was labeled Number One, the one at the south end Two, the numbering continuing clockwise up to Twelve.

"Well, well, what have we here?" a hearty voice announced, and Raber turned. "Hah! The police interested in what goes on at Twin Springs Trout Club!"

Gray-haired Thomas Larrimore was in his late fifties. The head of the Tax Department wore horn-rimmed glasses that decorated a red face, and his short stout body was clad in conventional business clothes.

"Refreshing my mind with the physical layout," Raber said.

"That all, eh? About time you investigated out there!"

"Isn't the trout fishing still superb?"

"What you don't know, captain! New owners, Empire Export and Import Company from New York City. Run by a city lawyer, Lawrence Oppenheim, a former guest at the club." Larrimore lowered his booming voice. "Strictly a fly-by-night outfit!"

"Really?"

"Wouldn't make the statement if it wasn't true." Larrimore waggled a pudgy finger. "Empire fooled the Barringtons, all right, but they don't fool yours truly!"

"Fly-by-night?" Raber repeated.

"Based on the sales contract, Barringtons and Empire. Now, total sales price seventy thousand dollars over real value. Why would Empire or Oppenheim pay such a ridiculous price, eh?"

"I have no idea."

"Because the down payment, cash in two installments, only totals fifty-four thousand! First installment, April first, twenty-seven thousand. Second installment, another twenty-seven thousand due October first. Also due on *that* date, eight percent interest on the hefty mortgage and a fat tax payment due on the borough." Larrimore waggled his fat forefinger again. "To summarize, captain, for a skimpy twenty-seven thousand dollars in cash, Empire acquired title to a valuable property. You know they operate a helicopter out there?"

"So I understand," Raber murmured. "Fly-by-night?"

"Captain, you just hold your horses! A copter's personal property, subject to borough taxation. So I investigated. Know what?"

Larrimore banged a fist against a palm.

"The copter's not subject to taxes, as it's rented from an outfit outside Trenton. Mark my word, before all those big payments come due, October first, Empire takes off in that rented copter for parts unknown! Captain, you better protect the Barringtons and the borough from being gyped!"

"What's the club's gross income per year?" Raber asked.

"Big, at least sixty thousand dollars."

"Isn't this a civil matter, Mr. Larrimore?"

"Not with the Barringtons and the borough about to be gyped!"

"Still a civil matter," Raber decided. "By spacing the cash

payments over a period of years, the Barringtons profited by paying considerably less in capital gains tax, correct?"

"Well—"

"Which makes it a profitable deal for the Barringtons. Deduct the initial cash payment, twenty-seven thousand, from a gross income of sixty thousand. Deduct interest charges on the mortgage. Add current expenses, plus six months' salaries for five employees. Obviously, no point in Empire running out prematurely with the property so valuable. Why won't they hang in there for the long-term profit, Mr. Larrimore?"

"Fly-by-night gyps!" Larrimore snorted, and leaned closer. "They bring in foreign fishermen and clean up!"

"Empire makes a higher profit from foreigners than from Americans?"

"They must!" Larrimore stared at Raber. "Seems to me you don't want to take action. Maybe I better go upstairs, eh?"

"Suit yourself."

"Well, you gotta take action on this! At Twin Springs, Empire operates an open whorehouse!"

"Really?"

"Whores for wealthy fishermen, Empire takes a big cut!"

"Any proof?" Raber asked.

"Sam Raymond told me that last week!"

"Mr. Raymond has firsthand evidence?"

"He got it from Billy Burkeson, the bartender at Fair Hills Tavern."

"Billy has firsthand evidence?"

"Billy heard it from two guests at Twin Springs. They stopped in for drinks. Always four or five whores out there! Captain, you gotta stop that in our borough!"

"You offer hearsay evidence, Mr. Larrimore, inadmissible in a court." Raber smiled reflectively. "Assume your facts are correct. Twin Springs is private property. We investigate and question an attractive young woman in residence with an older man. How do we establish she is a prostitute at work?"

"That's *your* job!"

"Ah, but she and he choose to remain silent. Or call in a

lawyer. Or say they are husband and wife." Raber shook his head. "We make asses of ourselves. If we receive a signed complaint, we go in. If *you* can prove management solicits prostitution business locally, we go in. That's it, Mr. Larrimore."

"Why'd you bust in here an' check those plat maps?"

"The Barringtons sold their jeep to Empire?" Raber countered.

"Yes!"

"Suppose the new owners failed to transfer ownership and obtain new plates for the jeep?"

"Penny-ante stuff!"

"Good morning," Raber said and started for the door.

"Captain, you gotta take action on this!"

Raber turned.

"September first the Water Department sent Jack Pelter to read the meter at Twin Springs! Joe Arragon, their new superintendent—he's a giant! Six-six, weight over two hundred fifty pounds! He won't let Pelter read the meter, beat the hell outa Pelter, and threw Pelter into a borough truck! Hah, what are you gonna do about *that?*"

"I'll check it for factual content, Mr. Larrimore," Raber replied pleasantly, and joined Mrs. Morrison in the anteroom where he said, "Thank you for the efficient arrangement of those plat maps."

"No trouble, captain." Nodding toward the inner office she hissed, "That old coot is off his rocker."

Downstairs in the Water Department, Raber waited while a flint-faced Miss Etting talked over a special shortwave hookup.

"Pelter bosses a leak in a water main," she explained stonily. "And what is *your* business with *him?*"

"*Our* business," Raber said, and strolled outside to the huge parking lot behind the building just as a work truck turned in and braked near Raber. A lightweight, Jack Pelter, jumped from the truck.

"Hey, good to see you, Freddy!" Pelter enthused, shaking hands. "We work for the same outfit, out of the same building, and never see each other." Sharp eyes ran over Raber.

"Man, do you look fit. Hear you box all the time at the YM."

"Bag punching, some sparring. Jack, how've you been?"

"No change since we were in high school together. Then, you could lick everybody. Later, when you fought professionally to pay the bills at college, I meant to ask you: When was it you fought Sugar Ray Robinson?"

"Don't be ridiculous, Jack."

"I keep hearin' the rumor. Any truth in it?"

"Probably started the summer after my freshman year at Rutgers," Raber suggested. "Sugar Ray had a training camp outside Suffern and needed sparring partners. I applied and they gave me a tough workout. I signed at a hundred a week. Man, I needed the money."

"And you *did* fight Sugar Ray?"

Raber laughed good-naturedly.

"Jack, I could always hit and they taught me finesse. It paid off later in club fights."

Pelter persisted. "Sugar Ray?"

"One of the finest gentlemen I ever met. They used to stage exhibitions and charged admission to help defray training expenses. You know, six-rounders. Three sparring partners, two rounds each. One Sunday a regular partner was sick and I substituted."

"Hey, you *did* fight Sugar Ray!"

"Nope, he carried me for two rounds. Jack, you're a water department foreman. Ever read any meters?"

"Yeah, oney big users. Fifteen, every three months."

"September first, did you read the meter at Twin Springs?"

"Sure, they got this four-inch main in from Haycock Road. They use our artesian water at the farmhouse, for the breeding pools an' all them lodges. That's why you pulled me in?"

"Right. You met a Joe Arragon out there?"

"Yeah."

"How big is he?"

"Maybe six-one, two-ten pounds."

"Arragon beat hell out of you and tossed you aboard a truck?"

"Freddy, who fed you that crap?"

"Tom Larrimore, just now in the Tax Office."

"Huh, that old fat frog!"

"Jack, what did happen out there on September first?"

"First, you remember that if Larrimore owned a pail of water he'd call it a water department." Pelter chuckled. "I go in like always, toot the horn three times. I lift the cellar door an' sing out: 'Water Department.' I start down the steps. Jeez, two big hands pick me up an' stand me against this truck. It's this Arragon, saying nobody goes in that cellar. I holler I read the meter or I shut off their water. He says try again an' he throws me over this truck. Freddy, I don't back off from no big SOB. I quick grab a long wrench from a toolbox. You know, the kind the fire guys use to turn on a fire hydrant. I yell I read the meter or I take that wrench an' trot out to Haycock an' turn off their goddamn water. All the yellin' fetches an old coot—uh, guy—named Palan, runs their office. I tell him I read that meter or I shut off their water with that wrench an' put 'em outa business. Hell, the waterlines are below frost level. To shut 'em off you gotta use a special long-handled—"

"I understand," Raber said. "Next?"

"Well, *they* don't know what *we* know! So Palan falls for the bluff an' shoos Arragon on his way. Cellar door's locked from the inside, see? Palan, he goes inside and unlocks it. So, I go in an' read their goddamn meter."

Pelter scratched his face.

"Why the hell keep that cellar door locked, huh? Oney change I see down there is a new petition, two padlocks on the door."

"Jack, why'd you grab that wrench in the first place?"

"That big SOB grabs me again I was gonna part his skull right down the middle, that's why." Pelter produced a limp cigarette, struck a long match with a fingernail, and fired the cigarette. "Freddy, those guys are from the big city. They come out here an' see all the grass an' trees an' birds an' they think we're stupid. Easy for us to fool 'em, see? They think that wrench shuts off their goddamn water main!"

"A good point to remember, Jack," Raber said.

"Partin' that big guy's skull with a wrench?"

"No, how easy for hicks to fool city people."

"Yeah." Pelter glanced at a wristwatch. "Gotta see that leak gets plugged." He swung aboard the truck, started the engine, and leaned from the cab. "Freddy, you can take that big Arragon easy."

"You plan to match us?"

"You never know. . . . The guy's muscle-bound."

At HQ, Raber asked Sprague, "Roy back?"

"With news. Nosse, license number on a green seventy-one Mustang?"

Nosse read from the log: "12-B-862, New Jersey."

"Owner and address?"

"General Sales Company, 1326 McCarter Boulevard, Newark."

Sprague continued: "Roy tailed Shellenbach down Broad to West Shopping Center where the smart aleck parked by an outside phone booth. He used a coin to raise the operator, then a charge card to talk for five minutes. He left by a side entrance, hit Harristown Road, and drove straight out to Twin Springs. Roy parked by the bridge on Haycock, got out, and lifted the hood. Shellenbach didn't stop at the office, but parked behind the lodge at the north end of the dam."

"Lodge One," Raber noted.

"He climbed the side steps and disappeared. Roy watched and fiddled with the engine. Seven minutes later Shellenbach walked along the dam wearing red swim trunks and carrying a fishing rod. That cured Roy's engine trouble and he drove home. Roy phoned General Sales in Newark and asked for Mr. Shellenbach. Said he had talked to the man and wanted to make a buy. A woman said Shellenbach was on vacation, but she was empowered to handle any stock transactions, so leave the order. Roy said he's wait for Shellenbach to return and broke the connection. We figure Shellenbach poses as a stock salesman at Twin Springs and General Sales is a cover for the cars in a private detective agency. I'm windy this morning, but you wanted a full make, captain?"

"I did."

"Roy raised the local super at Bell Tel and asked for the telephone number of Harry Shellenbach, probably in Essex County. Super said the number was unlisted, was this police business? Roy said all he wanted was the address. Nosse?"

Sande read off: "One twenty Lexington Street, Caldwell."

"A town north of Newark," Sprague explained.

"Where is Roy?" Raber asked.

"Right here," Boyce said, coming from the back area. "The lieutenant filled you in?"

"Capably. What's new?"

"Just talked to a Sergeant Anderson, Caldwell Police. August eleventh an officer ticketed Shellenbach for speeding at night. Next morning Shellenbach came in and pleaded for leniency. Anderson was on tour and knew the details. Shellenbach said he'd been tailing a hot suspect, a man with his fingers in his firm's till. He produced his private detective's license and substantiating data. For the log, Sande. Shellenbach's employer is Oliver Associates, a private detective agency in Newark. President, Gardner Oliver. Same address as General Sales, okay?"

"Quick, smart work."

"You want more, say smart aleck's shoe size?"

"We let it ride for the present," Raber decided.

"Well, I swan," Nosse said, and the three officers faced her. "An expression my Aunt Hilda uses. She's a hick like us. That's what she always says when she's surprised."

They all laughed.

3

AT HOME on Saturday morning, September 8, Fred Raber finished an early breakfast and leaned back at the kitchen table.

"Elise, another cup of your delicious coffee, please?"

She was two years younger than he and darkly demure. She replenished his cup from an electric percolator and she added half-and-half and one lump of sugar to suit his taste.

"Fred, is this as good as the girls brew at HQ?"

"Maybe a reasonable facsimile," he said teasingly. "What an improvement—they've perked up the entire squad, pun intended."

"When does Chief Hocking return from vacation?"

"Late tomorrow night to miss heavy traffic. Reports for duty on Monday, eight A.M."

"He certainly earned that vacation," she said jokingly. "Contending with you, comedian Parisi, and Angel-Face Boyce. After today you won't need to rush out of here at seven A.M. and arrive home God knows when, Captain Flatfoot."

"Oh, it hasn't been *that* bad."

"Just plenty of overtime, but never any overtime pay for the rank of captain." She made a face, cocked one ear. "Do I hear two little ones padding around upstairs?" She shook her head. "False alarm. Will I be happy when they both reach school age! And by the way, captain. Today is your day off, the weather is warm and beautiful. A thought, just the four of us. Off on a picnic at noon?"

"Great idea," he said approvingly. "Dick Sprague has the desk, he's a real take-charge officer, and—"

The telephone rang.

"Someday I'll throttle that gadget," Elise promised.

"Nothing interferes with the picnic," Raber said as he picked up the receiver.

"Raber here.... Yes, Grace.... No matter, anonymous or not. Where's Montanez? Turn him around on Vine and send him in. Last mile, full siren. Issue the order—I'll think."

He sat relaxed, a free hand picking up a light jacket draped over the back of a table chair.

Then: "Very good, Grace. Code everything *Hicksville*. Confirmation or not, we go in full strength. Route Boyce out of bed. He has no siren on his car, so he comes in with horn blasting and brakes squealing. Raise Lieutenant Sprague. Tell him to get in uniform and to take charge at the front building. And to come in siren open. I'm leaving now. Pick me up with news en route. Keep cool, honey."

In fluid motions he cradled the phone, pulled car keys from a pocket, draped the coat over an arm, and rose.

"An anonymous caller. Man drowned."

"Why the army on the move?" his wife asked.

"A chance to probe 'em," he flung over a shoulder.

"Where, where?"

From the living room he called back, "Twin Springs."

He was out the door, down the steps, and striding through the warm morning to the unmarked car parked nose-out in the driveway. He unlocked the door, flung the coat on the seat, slid behind the wheel, and started the engine. He hit the street in low gear, swung left, and shifted into high. Two blocks later he headed for the south extension of Harristown Road. At that intersection, as he turned north, Officer Gladwyn caught him.

"Captain Raber, respond please."

Driving with one hand, he grabbed the mike, pressed a button. "Let's hear it."

"Confirmation, male Caucasian. As yet, no age or other info. Wait a sec.... Monty says trouble!"

"Relax, he'll hear my siren. Notify county medical examiner. Press for an exact arrival time. Out."

Short of Broad Street he hit the siren and brakes, shot across as there was no traffic. Along Harristown Road he hit sixty miles an hour, the siren keening for Monty's benefit.

After a left turn into Haycock Road he cut the siren and upped the speed past sixty on the curling run past farms, woods, and a small housing development. At the bridge over the outlet brook from the pond he braked sharply and swung between stone pillars to enter the club's property.

No need to rush now.

At the north end of the dam, a squad car stood with the left front door open. Montanez was leaning inside and talking over shortwave. In a knot on the lane stood three men, all of them husky.

Raber angled left into a parking area below and behind Lodge One and stopped alongside a green Mustang. Carrying his jacket, he left the car. A hundred feet distant, beyond the waterfall, behind Lodge Two, stood a yellow MG dwarfed by a blue Continental, the latter sleek and new. He slipped on the jacket to free his arms, but mainly to conceal the .357 Magnum in its belt holster.

Lodge One sat atop a high foundation of cut stones. As he rounded the corner, headed for the stairs, he collided with a big man. He backed off, eyeing first dirty sneakers, then unbelted blue jeans, a tight T-shirt, a big-jawed face, and a head topped by short blond hair.

"Jeez, you scairt me!" Raber blurted, slipping easily into the Hicksville code, as he figured he had met Joe Arragon.

"Sonny, get back in that heap."

The voice was low-keyed, slow and soft, nothing at all as Raber had expected.

"Private property," the man continued. "Sonny, move it. Or I toss you and that heap into Haycock Road."

"Says who, buster?"

"Says Joe Arragon, superintendent. Move, sonny."

"Not a chance, I'm a cop."

"Show the ident, cop."

Raber fumbled in his jacket pockets.

"Got the badge somewhere, buster."

He tried the right pants pocket.

"Where'd I put it, huh?"

Triumphantly, he pulled a badge from his left pants

pocket. He placed a thumb over *captain*, shoved the badge under Arragon's nose.

"Fair Hills cop, that's me."

"Okay." Arragon's voice remained soft and calm. "You empty coins from parking meters maybe?"

"Yeah."

Along Haycock Road a car roared in, horn blaring. Brakes shrieked in protest and tires squealed.

"Who's the nut?" Arragon asked mildly.

"One tough cop, buster. Don't mess with him."

Roy Boyce slammed to a stop behind the Mustang. His car's front window was fully lowered on the right side. Feetfirst, Boyce simply slid through the window and hit the ground running.

"Pal, this tub a-lard givin' you trouble?"

"Says he's the super," Raber drawled. "Hell of a super, you ask me. The stupe let a man drown."

Arragon began: "I had nothing to do with—"

"Shuddup!" Boyce growled, patting the butt of his holstered Magnum. "Back off or you want a bullet in the belly button?"

Arragon stepped back. The two officers started up the stairs.

"You overplay the code," Raber chided.

"I shoulda been a stand-up comic." They paused short of the dam. "On the road, who's black mustache and the two goons?"

"Monty will know."

"Hah, he's got his Spanish up!"

By the squad car, in full uniform, Frank Montanez stood spread-legged, one thumb hooked in a cartridge belt and his dark eyes afire.

Left of the car, in a corner of the pond, thirty feet from the dam, snagged in reeds, face down, floated the body of a man who wore only red swim trunks. At several spots, on the perimeter of the pond, stood small groups of spectators, obviously guest fishermen.

"Easy, Monty," Raber soothed. "Data first, please."

"Just shot it to HQ," Montanez snapped, and handed a memo to Raber. "I came in fast, siren open. Those big bastards—"

Raber ordered, "Cool it," and began to read the memo aloud, softly: "Victim, male Caucasian. Guest, Lodge One. Harry Shellenbach, Newark, New Jersey. Stock salesman. No age listed on registration form. Discovered, floating in pond, six fifty A.M. By Werner DeHaven, building contractor. Guest, with Mrs. DeHaven, Lodge Two. More details available at office."

"Black mustache talked to the two goons, and they headed toward the farmhouse. Here comes mustache," Boyce whispered.

Raber pocketed the memo, wheeling toward the lane.

"Who are you?" he growled to a man in his mid-fifties.

"Gene Palan, officer."

"Your job here?"

"Officer, I'm in charge of the office."

"Okay, wait on the road."

Raber turned to Montanez. "Let's have it."

"I rolled in," the officer said calmly, "parked here, and spotted the corpse. I alerted Gladwyn. Joe Arragon stood on the dam. He boarded that small boat and started to row to the corpse. I ordered him back, but he disobeyed. I heard steps, and those two big goons were at my back. I said go back to the road, but they didn't move. I told Gladwyn *trouble*. Arragon was by the corpse, the two goons refused to budge. So I drew the .38 and the goons moved. Arragon had a rope and started to tie a noose. I told him only the medical examiner could touch that corpse. He said to go screw myself. I placed a shot left of the boat. The shot bounced off the water and the echoes sounded like the rattle of small fire. You bet he paddled for shore. Black mustache, Mr. Palan, pulled up and wanted to know about all the shooting. I told him what I told Arragon. Arragon walked up and said he was going to spank my ass, then toss me over Lodge One. Mr. Palan's a good guy and he told Arragon to guard the steps by Lodge One. Arragon left and Mr. Palan fed me the data. Captain, may I return here out of uniform and see if Arragon can spank my ass?"

"You know better than that," Raber said. "Arragon was out of line, you acted correctly. Raise Gladwyn. Send your replacement here at eight o'clock. Find out if she has an arrival time for the ME."

"Right, captain."

"Roy," Raber continued, "starting at this lodge the numbers continue clockwise up to twelve. I'll handle the DeHavens in Two. Use your car. Drift past Two, memorize the license numbers on that yellow MG and Lincoln Continental. Give me a memo and I'll run a make on them from HQ. Still 'Hicksville.' Briefly question the guests at Lodge Three. Who knew Shellenbach, how good a swimmer, any unusual noises last night at the pond, etcetera. We meet at Lodge Twelve. Is a half hour sufficient time?"

Raber said, "On the dot," strolled down the stairs, then summoned Palan.

"Sorry I blew my stack, bud, but Arragon don't cooperate with the officer in charge, see?"

"No reason for Arragon to be fired at!" Palan protested.

"You wait a tick-tock, bud. Our officer don't fire *at* Arragon." Something in Palan's manner temporarily eluded Raber. "Our officer is a crack shot with that peashooter. He fires *at* Arragon an' we got two bodies in the drink, see?"

"Still upsetting. Frankly, I dislike all violence."

"My apologies. When you last seen this Shellenbark?"

"*Shellenbach*," Palan corrected acidly. "Yesterday afternoon."

"Not last night, huh?"

"Last night I was asleep by ten o'clock."

"Who seen Shellenbark last? I mean *last* night."

"Probably our chef, Diego Ramose," Palan explained. "At Mr. Shellenbach's request, the chef broiled a trout. He delivered the trout personally to Lodge One at eight o'clock."

"Hah, he's drunk!"

"You mean the chef or Mr. Shellenbach?"

"The corpse—drunk. How else he falls in the drink an' drowns?"

"I haven't the slightest idea, officer."

Somewhere on Haycock a siren began to wail.

Palan moaned. "Please, not any more!"

"Lieutenant Sprague comin' in. He's the boss."

"He gotta make that infernal racket?"

"He don't get many chances to use a siren." Raber stifled a yawn. "Wait till the cowboys roll in, Mr. Palan."

"*Cowboys?*"

"Yeah, county patrolmen escortin' the ME an' ambulance. They wear Stetson hats. Cowboys, see? That's a joke."

"Officer, will there be reporters on the scene?"

"Don't worry about no bad publicity for the club, Mr. Palan. Shellenbark is oney a stat."

"*Stat?*" Palan echoed.

"Local police report all drownings, auto accidents, and other bodies to the county to total. This corpse becomes oney a statistic."

In front of the farmhouse the siren stopped its keening.

"Mr. Palan, be a good boy. See the lieutenant gets fed breakfast. He come out here empty bellied."

Palan hurried down the lane.

"Now we're Keystone Kops?" Montanez drawled.

"I laid it on too thick?"

"Yes, captain. My relief is driving directly here. It's not the ME on the way. An assistant, Dr. Wightman, probably arrived by eight A.M."

"Good. I'll question the DeHavens in Lodge Two. See that nobody enters Lodge One. And make sure Shellenbach's Mustang is locked."

"As ordered, captain."

Near the spillway, Raber fingered the water, found it tepid. Since warmth slowed the action of rigor mortis, this might pose a problem for Dr. Wightman in determining the actual time of death. However, a broiled trout consumed about eight o'clock last night? That item loomed more important in the time sequence of events last night.

Raber crossed the spillway on a plank. A one-inch-deep

overflow resulted in a steady, musical waterfall in a twenty-foot drop.

Presiding over a cup of coffee and an electric percolator, Werner DeHaven sat on the wide porch at Lodge Two, at a table under the roof's low overhang. He had cropped black hair, intense black eyes, and a strong, tanned face. Wide through the shoulders, his thick, hairy arms protruded from the short sleeves of an unbuttoned blue silk shirt. More hair matted his chest. He wore shorts and sneakers and exuded the aura of a muscleman who wore two other discernible labels—money and success.

"Fred Raber in this corner, sir. Fair Hills Police. Guess you must be Werner Haven, right?"

"DeHaven," the man growled.

Raber pulled a memo from a jacket pocket and studied it.

"Yeah, DeHaven. You alone here?"

"I am alone *here*."

"What about Mrs. DeHaven?"

"Inside dressing."

"She available maybe?"

"After she dresses. How in hell could she sleep during all the unnecessary police racket?"

"This memo says you found the corpse, right?" Raber said.

"Correct."

"Who phoned the alert to the police?"

"I did."

Raber pocketed the memo. "Why make it anonymous?"

"Certainly that was not my intention."

"Look, don't snap at me, I'm oney part of routine. I gotta fill out a report. An' I forgot my notebook. Okay to cut cross-lots?"

DeHaven stared.

"Raber, what does 'cross-lots' mean?"

"Keep it short, just the main parts. Start when you rolled outa bed. Run it to here, okay?"

DeHaven paused to drain his coffee, then refilled the empty cup.

"I'm an expert fisherman," he clipped off. "Means I start very early to hook into the big ones. The alarm rang at five

27

thirty. I shut it off. Mrs. DeHaven likes to sleep late. I dressed and selected my gear. I walked out here. This is a porch. Over to the left—see the dock?—Lodge Three, where I started to fish. I cast a hundred feet. See the dark water? *Dark* indicates the deepest water. Where the biggest trout lurk. I started to work this way and—"

"Sun up in the east?"

"Raber, the sun always rises in the east!"

"I mean, light enough to see red trunks on that corpse?"

"You want this story my way or yours?"

"Sorry, you're the big boss."

"I fished with dry flies. What is a dry fly? It floats on top of the water. Does a dry fly become wet? Yes, so what does one do? He replaces the *wet* dry fly with a new dry fly. He hooks the wet fly in his hat to dry. That takes time. The casts are still long. An hour passed. If you jot no notes, Raber, how are you going to write your report?"

"Oh, I got this photoelectric brain."

"You have *what?*"

"Look, you been fishin' over an hour an' don' catch the corpse."

"Jesus, Joseph, and Mary!" DeHaven exploded, clenching both big hands convulsively. "I reached the spillway! I crossed on the plank! I spotted the floating corpse! It was Harry Shellenbach and—"

"Knew him right off?"

"Shellenbach arrived on Monday morning! We were close neighbors for five days! He always wore red swim trunks! So I knew—"

"Don't blow a gasket."

DeHaven came up off the chair.

"Officer of the law, get this! One more crack out of you and in the pond you go! Understand?"

"Yes, sir," Raber agreed, having obtained what he wanted to know—that this was a powerful man with a short fuse on a hot temper.

Ten seconds drifted past.

"Shellenbach floated very still," DeHaven continued, his voice calm. "I knew he was dead. I dropped my rod on the

28

dam. Each lodge has a telephone, but all calls pass through a central switchboard in the main office at the farmhouse. I doubted Mr. Palan was up. The chef was, there was smoke from the chimney on the farmhouse. I ran into the kitchen and told the chef that Shellenbach had drowned, to call Mr. Palan. I continued to the front of the farmhouse and entered the office. I raised the operator and told her: *Emergency, connect me with the Fair Hills Police Department.* She insisted I supply my telephone number and I gave her that of the club's. She connected me with the police and your female officer answered: *Officer Gladwyn, Fair Hills Police.* I said: *Man drowned, pond. Twin Springs Trout Club. You have the message?* She repeated it and I broke the connection."

DeHaven stared at Raber.

"You interpret that as an anonymous telephone call?"

"Forget it, sir. Next?"

"I returned to the dam and recovered my rod. Arragon arrived first, followed by Mr. Palan and the chef. Then the helicopter pilot and Paul Goodone. Count them, Raber, five employees. I returned here to wait. A siren sounded on Haycock Road. So, I witnessed the ensuing police stupidity."

"Strong word, sir."

"That stupid cop shot at Joe Arragon!"

"You mean Officer Montanez, a crack shot," Raber said mildly. "Only the medical examiner may touch that corpse, that's the law. Three times Arragon disobeyed the officer's orders."

"That cop should have tried something else!"

"Such as?"

"Not shooting!"

"Swimmin' out, maybe?"

"I told my story!" DeHaven flared. "You didn't bother to take a single note!"

"Told you, forgot my notebook." Raber jerked a thumb toward the screened door. "She dressed yet?"

DeHaven called out: "Honey!"

From just inside the door a woman answered, "Coming, darling," and the screen door swung outward.

She was thirty years old, Raber decided. Or, twenty years

younger than DeHaven. A statuesque blonde with blue eyes and blond hair, wearing an expensive blue linen suit with a yellow blouse and blue high-heeled slippers.

"Yes?" she asked DeHaven.

"Raber, Fair Hills Police," DeHaven explained. "He insists on questioning you about the drowning."

"Good morning, Officer Raber," she said, smiling. "May I help you?"

"Golly, I hope so. What is your name, please?"

"Oh, for crissakes," DeHaven snorted, but the woman said, "I am Mrs. DeHaven, of course."

"Gotta fix the time of drownin', Mrs. DeHaven. Last night, what time does everybody hit the sack?"

"Mr. DeHaven very early, ten o'clock. I read for a while until eleven o'clock."

"Hear splashes in the pond, maybe a yell for help?"

"No, the windows were open, it was unusually quiet."

"How good a swimmer was this Shellenbach?"

"Ummm, for five days I saw the man frequently. Generally he wore red swim trunks, no other color. Frankly, I never recall seeing him *in* the water. You, darling?"

"I saw him *once* in the water. Six fifty this morning."

"A Miss Evelyn Noornan," she continued, "knows much more about Mr. Shellenbach than we. For five days she practically lived with him."

"Shacked up in Lodge One?"

A ghost of a smile crossed her lovely face.

"Officer Raber, I intended no such connotation. Miss Noornan resided in Lodge Twelve. The two were together constantly. Fishing from the dam or a boat. Walking the road and—"

"Jayne!" DeHaven interrupted.

"Darling, I'm merely indicating the situation to Officer Raber. They visited at both lodges, cocktails, and—"

"Stow it!" DeHaven growled. "Finished, Raber?"

"Sure am," Raber said cheerfully. "Glad to finish the routine. Very nice meeting you, Mrs. DeHaven. Mr. DeHaven, my pleasure. I'll have a steno type out your story.

Fetch it out later for you to sign and complete the investigation."

As Raber strolled across the dam, DeHaven snapped, "Good riddance to a clown!"

"Darling, no point in remaining upset."

"Reporters may be along any minute. We can't risk their sharp questioning. Your bags packed?"

"Of course."

"When that clown heads up to Lodge Twelve, slip off in the MG. Okay to breakfast on the way home?"

"Of course, darling."

DeHaven rose and followed her into the lodge.

4

INSIDE THE squad car, Montanez sat relaxed.

As Raber arrived, he warned, "We're under surveillance, captain. The big guy on the chair behind the barn. You left, he arrived with coffee and a newspaper. I swiveled the rear mirror to keep tabs. Coffee's gone and the newspaper's only window trimming."

"Good work. Dr. Wightman still arriving at seven fifty?"

"Definite. The Mustang's locked."

"Keep faking the nap act. Can you see the parking lot behind Lodge Two, clearly the yellow MG and blue Lincoln Continental?"

"Yes."

"Expect action there shortly. I'm meeting Roy at Lodge Twelve."

Without glancing at the floating corpse, Raber strolled off. As he started up the lane, he ignored the watcher. Beyond the barn, extending toward the farmhouse, were two rectangular trout-breeding pools, close together, fifteen by sixty feet, each fed by a spurting fountain. In both shallow waters, hundreds of dark shapes moved restlessly.

At right angles to the pools and parallel to the farmhouse, stood a long one-story structure with a low, peaked roof. An unused horse stable it featured six stalls with Dutch doors, each door consisting of two units divided horizontally. None of the units were completely closed and one door near the center was completely open on sagging hinges.

Raber mounted the road through scattered tall red oaks, glimpsing a parking area behind Lodge Twelve, then followed a path to the wide porch. Behind a screened door a solid door stood closed. At windows on either side, however, the sashes were raised behind screens. He noted the watcher following his movements, so he moved to the door where he could not be observed.

He rapped on the doorjamb. Inside the lodge echoes ran around hollowly. He waited ten seconds, then rapped a second time, more sharply. Still no response. He tested the screen door and found it unlocked. Easing this door open several inches, he reached one hand in, turned the knob on the solid door, and pushed gently. The door was unlocked. Quietly he reclosed both doors, then strode along the porch, intending to check the rear parking area for a car.

"Nobody home!" the watcher called up.

"Just checkin' out all lodges," Raber called back. "Oney routine. You work here, bud?"

"Yeah."

"Name of the guests?"

"One woman, a Miss Noornan. Mr. Palan said she left last night and drove home."

"When's the dame due back?"

The watcher growled, "Ask Palan," and returned to his paper.

By his wristwatch, Raber noted the time, seven fifty-five. He sat on the porch, shoes resting on the path. In front of Lodge Eleven Boyce stood and chatted with a tall man wearing tan shorts. When Boyce semisaluted and started toward Lodge Twelve, Raber walked forward and met him at the road.

"Don't look at the watcher behind the barn," he warned softly.

Boyce handed over a memo which Raber pocketed.

"License numbers, on the MG and Lincoln," Boyce whispered. "Lodge Two?"

"I think Tom Larrimore, Tax Office, is probably correct—a call-girl racket here. A woman twenty years younger than Werner DeHaven introduces herself as his wife, but I'm sure she lied. You?"

"Guests in the other lodges knew Shellenbach by sight," Boyce explained. "Identifying characteristic, almost always wearing a pair of red swim trunks. Odd, though. Nobody remembered seeing him swimming by the dam."

"So I was told at Lodge Two."

"Last night no guests heard any unusual noises, say splashing in the pond, somebody diving in, or a muffled cry for help. A young couple in Lodge Seven have a porch close to the water. Married, name of Rogers. Both in advertising, here for fishing and relaxation. They sat on that porch last night until they heard the bell in the Baptist church in town ring twelve times. Any unusual sounds from the direction of Lodge Two would have been amplified off the water, but they heard nothing unusual and I believed them. The tall character in Lodge Eleven, a Mr. Grayfield, is from Ridgefield, Connecticut. Been coming here for eight seasons and knows everybody. Lodge Ten's empty, Grayfield said it had been occupied for several days by three foreign fishermen—an Englishman, an Irishman, no nationality for the third. Yesterday afternoon they were ferried in the helicopter to International Airport, Philly, return flight, Pan Am, to Shannon Airport. In Lodge Twelve, any contributions from the interesting Miss Evelyn Noornan?"

"That watcher yelled she drove home sometime last night."

"Fred, rate her our best witness," Boyce advised. "Grayfield knows her very well, she's a regular guest. Practically drooled over her. Thirty-one or two, unmarried, expert fisherman. Brunette. Rather tall, five-eight. Body beautiful, really stacked in the bikinis she liked to wear. Grayfield knew Shellenbach arrived Monday morning. He said the two first met that day on the dam before Lodge One, became good friends. Also noted Shellenbach was a poor fisherman, never swam by the dam, but Noornan did. The two were inseparable. Fishing, walking, drinking, and dining together. Oh—Grayfield said Shellenbach occasionally snapped photos of the woman poised on the dam. If you wonder why Grayfield went into all the detail, I rate him as the jealous type. What do you think?"

"It's important to locate Noornan and determine if Shellenbach could swim. She may be able to shed light on how he managed to get in that pond at least once—at night—and drown. This your day off?"

"Overtime?" Boyce countered.

Raber nodded and Boyce smiled like a cherub.

"I'm free except for payments on the new Ford and marriage in November. What's on your mind?"

"An assistant ME's due any moment. Afterward, I'll return to HQ. You stay; nobody goes inside Lodge One until I return. Last night at eight o'clock the chef delivered a broiled trout to Shellenbach, who was alone. Check the kitchen first. Was that trout eaten? If so, let me know immediately. Determine if there is any evidence to say Shellenbach drank heavily. Afterward, proceed as in murder one, minus pix and prints. Inventory and pack all the victim's personal possessions. Find his car keys. Stow the stuff in the Mustang, which gives you a chance to check whatever is inside, including the back seat."

"Noted, captain. Hah, the whirring brain! Dick Sprague's appraisal, Shellenbach, Thursday A.M., at HQ. *Not scared, but sweating, like he had bumped into something beyond his depth.* No pun, I didn't mean the pond water! That the reason for M-1 treatment?"

"Merely a precaution," Raber said. "Later, run a casual check on Palan. Still 'Hicksville.' Exact time Noornan left for home, possible reason for her departure, when and if she plans to return, plus her home address. Palan should cooperate."

"Anything else?"

"Yes, we give that man behind the barn a hard time."

They strolled down the slope to where the watcher still sat, apparently engrossed in a newspaper.

"This fellow told me he worked here," Raber said.

"Maybe he collects old newspapers," Boyce decided. "Sonny do you have a name?"

Glaring, the man growled, "I'm Carl Krauthof."

Boyce chuckled. "Krauthof means a cabbagehead in German. Cabbage head, what work do you do here?"

"I'm the fly-boy!"

"You tie flies on fishing lines for the guests?"

"Goddamnit, I pilot the helicopter!"

"ZOOM! Off into the wild blue yonder," Boyce jeered. "Fred, do you know how they operate this place?"

"Tell me," Raber suggested, stifling a yawn.

"Those two long trout pools are called raceways. One pool holds eight- to ten-inchers that are force-fed. When they grow up they're dumped into the second raceway. Guests can catch all the trout they want and just turn in the total lengths caught so the pond can be restocked. Why is the fishing so good? The pond is overstocked and those big trout are hungry. Hell, any kid with a bent pin on a fishline could hook into—"

On Haycock Road a siren began to keen.

"Here comes the parade!" Boyce enthused, and they moved toward the lane, followed by Krauthof.

Montanez had backed out the squad car, parked, and alighted.

Siren wailing, a county black-and-white appeared. "Cowboy at the wheel," Boyce announced happily. Next, a black county sedan. "The medical examiner," Boyce explained. Red lights winking, an ambulance followed with two white-clad attendants in the front seat. "To haul off the body," Boyce added. Then, a second county black-and-white, turret light winking. "Darn, end of parade," Boyce complained.

"Bunch of hicks," Krauthof grunted and returned to his chair.

Montanez waved the lead car farther up the road, motioned the ME to park in front of the local squad car, directed the ambulance to back to the dam, and held the fourth car below Lodge One. Boyce headed for Lodge One and Montanez joined Raber on the road.

"After you left," he reported, "there was some action at Lodge Two. A doll dressed in blue, nice legs, came out, went down to the MG, unlocked the left doors, left them open, and returned inside the lodge. At the rear, DeHaven sneaked behind the Lincoln, stowed a large suitcase and a smaller one into the rear of the MG, closed the rear door, repeated the sneak act, and disappeared behind the lodge. The doll reappeared, carrying a yellow strap-purse. She drove out the front entrance, captain, then toward town."

"Good work, Monty."

Dr. Wightman was a tall young man who wore horn-rimmed glasses.

"Nice meeting you, Dr. Wightman," Raber said politely. "Captain Raber, Fair Hills Police."

"Finally caught up with you," Wightman said, shaking hands. "I expected . . . okay, an older man. You have good friends in the county, Major Orwell and my superior, Dr. Hollender." Wightman readied a ball-point and notebook. "Preliminary data, please?"

Raber detailed personal items anent the victim, then added: "We have uncovered no facts as to how or when the victim drowned. On a warm night, no guests heard any unusual sounds from this area. One moment, please."

Notebook in hand, Boyce arrived from inside Lodge One. Raber made the introductions and the two younger men shook hands. "What about that trout?" Raber asked.

"One broiled trout delivered at this lodge," Boyce ticked off. "Last night, at eight o'clock, victim alone. Found one dirty plate, silverware for one, in the sink, all smelling of fish. Partial remains, one large trout, in a smelly garbage can that does not speak well for management's housekeeping."

"Got it," Wightman noted. "Anything else?"

"Doctor," Raber said, "we know the victim was in the midst of a drink when the chef delivered the broiled trout. Roy?"

"Victim in residence five days," Boyce explained. "Again, poor housekeeping. In a very large, overflowing trash container in the kitchen, I found—let me read this." Boyce consulted his notebook. "One empty scotch bottle, Teacher's Highland Cream. One empty, Canadian Club whiskey. One empty, bottled martinis. One empty, bottled Manhattans. One empty, white wine, on an open shelf. Another Highland Cream, one-quarter filled. One Canadian Club, one inch left. One unopened bottle of red wine. Dr. Wightman, we are quite sure that the victim had some drinking assistance from a female guest."

"Still a lot of liquor for the time period," he said, closing his notebook. "Thank you, officer. I'll run a check on the alcoholic content of the victim's blood."

As Boyce started toward Lodge One, Raber asked, "You plan to do a complete autopsy?"

"Ummm, anything particular in mind, captain?"

"I would appreciate an analysis of the water in the victim's lungs as against a sample of the pond water."

"That is—" Wightman paused. "Why, captain?"

"I like thoroughness."

"You—like—" Again Wightman paused. "Why did you mention that last word?"

"Sorry, no criticism intended whatsoever."

"Captain, I've been given to understand you know *your* job. I suggest you extend the same courtesy to me."

Wightman wheeled to the two ambulance attendants.

"Don't stand there and gawk! Get blankets and a stretcher! And somebody better know how to paddle that boat!"

They went into action and Raber returned to the unmarked car behind Lodge One.

5

AT POLICE headquarters Officer Sande Nosse manned the desk alone since Lieutenant Sprague was still occupied at Twin Springs.

"Everything under control?" Raber asked.

"It's been rather quiet, captain." Her lovely face clouded. "I feel sorry for poor Mr. Shellenbach."

In a few months, Raber knew, one of the three probationary female officers would be promoted to the rank of detective second-grade, and he wondered if Nosse were too soft for the job.

"How did that poor man drown?" she asked.

"We know very little," Raber answered, then brutally: "He floated in that pond for hours. His skin was shriveled and puckered. Big trout had nibbled on his flesh."

She turned pale.

He snapped, "This is no time for sentimentality," and handed her a memo. "Those are the license numbers for two strange cars. You have three minutes for the full makes."

He strode into the rear area and phoned his wife to explain that the proposed picnic was out. He spoke next to his son, then to his daughter. At the expiration of three minutes he closed the conversation and returned to the front room.

Nosse handed over a neat memo with the terse comment, "Captain, I procured all the pertinent information," and he decided she had a quality or two that a good detective needed.

First item:
Lincoln sedan, blue, 1974 model
License number: X 28-071, N.J.
Owner: DeHaven Construction Company,
2076 Plank Road, Newark, N.J.

The obvious interpretation—the Lincoln was part of the company fleet and carried on the books as a tax writeoff.

Second item:
MG, yellow, '72 model
License number: BDR-741, N.J.
Owner: Jayne L. Lorning
Address: Highline Apartments,
23 Addison Place, Newark, N.J.

He wrote down the Lorning address in a notebook.

He ordered, "Dictation," and Nosse stood in readiness. "Prepare a new file, marked Harry Shellenbach, address from log. Type and file all log info. Next, a deposition form for Werner DeHaven, address from Lincoln sedan. Single space, one carbon. Place, Twin Springs Trout Club, town. DeHaven, guest occupant, Lodge Two. Note: Adjacent to Lodge One, occupied by Harry Shellenbach. Victim discovered in pond, approximately six fifty A.M., September eighth, by Werner DeHaven while fishing from shore. DeHaven personally telephoned the FHPD of the body, call received by Officer Gladwyn. At the conclusion, a place for the time deposition is signed, DeHaven's signature and mine, but do not attach my official title."

Next, Raber dictated the story that DeHaven had offered earlier on the porch at Lodge Two.

After a moment Raber continued: "I'm heading for Newark. Give me a half-hour start, then phone Oliver Associates, Newark, address from log, Thursday. They should have a standby or monitor service. Message: *Captain Raber, FHPD, on way to Newark. Urgent he meet top man, Oliver Associates, their office, at ten thirty this morning.* Use diplomacy and firmness. You know nothing that is in Captain Raber's mind or the reason for the urgency. Reason for *you*: I want to jolt their top man. That's it, thank you."

Nosse glanced up from her notes.

"Here's a personal comment, Sande. You're new at this game, so accept an apology for my earlier brusqueness. We all must cry at times, but generally a mask hides our sympathetic hearts so that we can maintain an objective attitude. The idea is to select the appropriate time for tears, understand?"

"Yes, captain."

"Lieutenant Sprague will return later, then more typing for the Shellenbach file. Detective Boyce is staying at Twin Springs. If anyone inquires, I am out. Bye, honey."

"Good hunting, captain," Nosse said.

As he started the unmarked car, he remembered an unfortunate incident: the use of the word "thoroughness" to Dr. Wightman.

Consequently, he parked at the main entrance of the Municipal Building, strode downstairs to the Water Department, and obtained a copy of the latest analysis of the local artesian water supply. He stowed this, an "in case item," in his wallet and headed for Newark.

Highline Apartments was a huge, three-building complex on Addison Place in the vicinity of the Lackawanna-Erie Railroad Station. At a desk in the central lobby, Raber identified himself to a clerk and received the information that a Mrs. Jayne L. Lorning was in residence, Apartment 1418, B-complex, and was this police business?

Raber said, "Just an unsettled traffic ticket and I happen to be in Newark this morning," and followed arrows and a tunnel into B-complex where he used a self-service elevator to reach the fourteenth floor. More arrows and hallways led him to the door of 1418 where he knocked and received no answer. He knocked again.

Then he heard a familiar female voice somewhere on a nearby hallway. He strode to another door and stood there as if he had just knocked. Mrs. Lorning entered the hallway, followed by a uniformed porter who carried a large suitcase and a smaller one. Mrs. Lorning unlocked 1418 and the two disappeared inside. A minute after the porter left, Raber knocked again. Almost immediately the door opened the length of a burglar chain.

She asked: "Who is—"

One eye stared and half of a mouth remained open.

Then she exclaimed: "My God, Officer Raber! What in the world are you doing here?"

"May I talk to you for a moment, please?"

The door closed, then reopened wide.

"Do come in," she said.

He inventoried a large, pleasant living room with a bank of curtained windows on the right, open doors into a bedroom and a lavatory on the left, and a glimpse of a kitchenette at the rear.

"Lovely place," he murmured politely.

"Why are you here?" she asked suspiciously. "Certainly not because I impressed you so deeply this morning!"

"May I say *you* impressed *me* deeply this morning—Mrs. Lorning."

"Damn. You know—of course you know my name! Or you wouldn't be inside my apartment."

She laughed a bit ruefully.

"And obviously you are not—well, the clown Werner and I thought you were. Do you have identification?"

From his left pants pocket Raber produced a badge which she studied and then exclaimed: "A captain!"

"Just lucky, Mrs. Lorning." He displayed his wallet and let her inspect his official commission. "Are you satisfied?"

"I didn't doubt your authority." She studied him coolly. "I'm just cautious."

"Mrs. Lorning, were you cautious at Lodge Two?"

"Touché."

She gestured to a divan under the windows.

"Let's sit there and be more comfortable."

He waited until she had seated herself on the divan and crossed the legs that Officer Montanez had earlier described as good, then faced her from the depths of an easy chair.

"Captain, how were you able to arrive here so quickly?"

"I drove down Route Seventeen in an unmarked police car. On your trip home did you stop for a leisurely breakfast?"

"I did. Why are you here?"

"That answer is more complicated. Do you object to bluntness?"

"I prefer it."

"When I question someone officially, I expect truthful answers. However, the police do expect to receive answers that circumvent the truth. I suspect that's our occupational hazard."

He smiled easily, in no hurry.

"You know, of course, that certain segments of society call us pigs and worse. Other people regard us as stupid, particularly after they receive traffic tickets they deserved. We live with derogatory appraisals and try to turn them to our advantage. If someone regards us as stupid, Mrs. Lorning, we gain an advantage."

"That explains your not-too-bright role at Lodge Two?"

He chuckled. "It does. After seven o'clock this morning there were four of us on the job at Twin Springs. If I deceived you, remember we deceived the employees."

"I think you did. Are you a college graduate?"

"Yes, Rutgers University. Now, the way we played our cards at Twin Springs has no direct connection with you or Mr. DeHaven. Right now, I believe the employees also regard the local police as stupid."

Raber leaned forward, his manner confidential.

"Mrs. Lorning, if you should telephone Mr. DeHaven from here, your call would pass through an office switchboard. If you tell him about the real me, your call may be monitored and we would lose the temporary advantage we have established, understand?"

"Of course. But I have no intention of telephoning Werner. He'll be here some time tomorrow afternoon." She gestured gracefully. "Are you going to explain why you are here?"

"Sorry, I was laying the groundwork. Is Mr. DeHaven married?"

"Yes."

"Several days ago—this, too, is confidential—we received a tip concerning the management at Twin Springs. I'll be blunt. Management supplies its wealthy guests with a top call-girl service. Personally, I am not a moralist. However, if the time comes when we receive a signed complaint, say an attempt to blackmail a guest, in we go. And I always like to have at least one ace behind my badge. Mrs. Lorning, you have my word. If you cooperate now, what you tell me remains confidential. At present, the furthest action from my mind would be to procure a court subpoena and drag you back to Fair Hills for questioning."

He paused thoughtfully.

"All I need, Mrs. Lorning, are several simple answers to several simple questions. Do you work for the management at Twin Springs?"

"No."

"Whenever management needed the services of a lovely lady, did it contact your employer?"

"No, somebody phoned my ex-employer."

"Did management receive a percentage of the charged fees?"

"Yes, a twenty percent cut."

"Mrs. Lorning, forget that I asked those questions. Now, what was Harry Shellenbach's vocation?"

"He told Werner he sold stocks and bonds."

"Did Mr. DeHaven ever comment on the man's fishing ability?"

She smiled. "Yes. Werner said he was terrible."

"We come to a long question," Raber told her. "Isn't it more than a coincidence that an inexpert fisherman paid the club's weekly rate of two hundred fifty dollars, arrived at Lodge One almost simultaneously with your and Mr. DeHaven's arrival at nearby Lodge Two, posed as a stock salesman when in fact he was a private detective?"

Her eyes widened.

"All I do is—is stare at you!"

"That's all right," he assured her. "Earlier you suggested that Evelyn Noornan—no, let that wait. Did Mr. DeHaven ever comment on her fishing ability?"

"He said she was expert!"

"Now I must be repetitive," Raber apologized. "When Evelyn Noornan swam near the dam did Shellenbach wear red swim trunks?"

"Always!"

"Yet you and Mr. DeHaven never saw him enter the water?"

"Not once."

"If Miss Noornan posed on the dam, did Mr. Shellenbach often seem to be snapping her picture?"

"Oh, that fink!" she exclaimed angrily. "Now I understand what he was up to, because we often sat very close on the porch of our lodge." She studied Raber carefully. "You're far ahead of Werner and me, captain. However, you have yet to explain how you learned my identity. Mind?"

"A good police officer is observant, Mrs. Lorning. When I arrived behind Lodge One and parked, I noticed near Lodge Two a yellow MG dwarfed by a blue Lincoln Continental. That suggested two disparate owners or drivers. The cars also suggested two disparate personalities, say a young woman for the MG and an older man. Couple those facts with our tip on a call-girl service. Later, I told our detective to memorize the license numbers of the two cars as he passed in his car on the way to interrogate the occupants of Lodge Three and—"

Raber snapped his fingers.

"I'm running to long sentences this morning. Later at headquarters the duty officer checked with the New Jersey Motor Vehicle Department and that's how your name and address surfaced."

"How simple!"

"It was a routine exercise, Mrs. Lorning. Mr. DeHaven is a rugged individual. He worked himself up from the bottom?"

"Yes, he started out as a bricklayer."

"He still exudes an aura of tremendous physical power," Raber said. "Does he have a short fuse on a hot temper?"

"Captain," she reproved, "don't put me on. This morning Werner disliked you. He kept you standing. He failed to offer you coffee. He lost his temper. Also, he told his story as if you were a child. You know he has a hot temper."

"I'm merely seeking corroboration, Mrs. Lorning, and that is fundamental in police work." Raber continued to speak casually. "Suppose Mr. DeHaven learned that Shellenbach was a detective who gathered divorce evidence.

Would Mr. DeHaven blow a fuse? Would he take some direct action? That is, would he overpower Shellenbach easily and hold the man's head under water until—"

She shot up off the divan, blue eyes ablaze, hands balled into fists.

Before she could explode, Raber said soothingly: "My dear, your reaction is the corroboration I sought. Please sit down."

"You're hinting that somebody drowned that horrid man?" she flared.

"Please—I merely ask questions. I assemble all the related facts and explore every possible explanation before drawing the inferences. Look at these facts. Everybody associated Shellenbach with those red swim trunks he always wore. No guest ever saw him enter the water. Last night no other guests heard unusual sounds near the pond. One couple sat pondside until after the church bell in Fair Hills tolled twelve o'clock. How and when did Shellenbach manage to drown? Was he drunk? Did he tumble accidentally into the deep water by Lodge One where the dam is narrow? Did he inhale a lungful of water before he could shout an SOS? During the day, why did Shellenbach avoid the water? Could he swim?"

Raber rose, sat on the divan, and patted her fists.

"The circumstances of the drowning elude me. I'm a cop doing a job and I promise not to fire any more stray shots."

"You fired that shot at Werner on purpose!"

"I apologize," he said, and stopped patting her fists. "In my book you are both interesting and attractive. So far we have been unable to locate Evelyn Noornan for questioning because she drove home sometime last night. When we do find her we hope she will be able to shed some light on the drowning."

Raber slid low on the divan, a picture of frustration.

"Frankly, Mrs. Lorning, we could take the easy way out. We forget the unfortunate circumstances and label the drowning an accident. Shellenbach is a stranger in town. But we do have pride and we do want to know. When I interrogate Evelyn Noornan, I want some solidity behind the badge. Perhaps you can be of help. That's why I came here, for no other reason. In this apartment, Mr. DeHaven can't gag you as he did earlier this morning and you are free to talk."

"I only said hello to the woman once," she protested.

"No matter. Listen while I ramble a bit." He chuckled as if he were amused. "On another case I interrogated a man who had lived for eighteen years with his wife. It developed that he was unaware of three of her salient characteristics. How had I learned them? From a woman who had met his wife just once and chatted for twenty minutes. It was as if she had looked into the wife's mind through an open window. You know the banality. One female poses no secret to another female. Care to give me a rundown on Evelyn Noornan?"

She sat in concentrated thought, then said, "Very well, but this is my opinion, not evidence."

As she began to talk, Raber closed his eyes.

"Evelyn Noornan is in her early thirties, say thirty-two. She stands five-eight, an inch taller than Shellenbach. Make her weight a hundred thirty pounds. Werner said she is single. She's a brunette and paraded around in—no, flaunted herself—in a bikini, a different one each day and all expensive. She is really stacked, but her knees are a bit knobby and her waist out of proper proportion to the bust and hips. She's a seal in the water. When she moved about on the dam, she exhibited quickness and seemed to have abnormal strength for a woman. Perhaps she has had karate training. If you get fresh with her, *powie!* But why come to *me* for information?"

"Because I want to meet her," Raber said, eyes still closed.

"You have, her physical self. Now her salient characteristics? Most women are curious, even nosy like myself, and I suspect Noornan is nosy. Look at this incident. About two P.M. on Monday, his first day at the club, Shellenbach fished from the dam. Werner pointed out his clumsiness, but I was uninterested. I had spotted Noornan standing on the lane below Lodge Twelve. She wore a bikini, what else? Shellenbach hooked into a trout and she hurried down the lane. Werner laughed at the man's inexpertise and Noornan must have been aware of that, also. He knelt to net the trout. Noornan arrived and said something and his eyes ran up that lush figure. I rated Shellenbach less than an average man, not worth a second look. They talked briefly and she knelt beside him. You know, her nudity against his bareness and she must have set him on fire. She unhooked the trout and tossed it into the pond. Werner said it was a peewee. They talked. They entered Lodge One. Captain, are you asleep?"

She's sharp, Raber thought and said aloud, "I'm fascinated."

"A half hour later, Noornan walked alone up to Lodge Twelve where she was staying. At six o'clock, dressed casually, Shellenbach hurried up to Twelve. With Werner and me, things are relaxed. I dislike fishing and had time for observation. We had cocktails and I prepared a light meal. Afterward, Werner catnapped in the main room, as usual, because he'd gone fishing very early. At eight o'clock, those two walked down from Lodge Twelve. Noornan wore a tennis outfit and they entered Lodge One. I gave them a few minutes. Werner was still sleeping. He has binoculars that he uses to scan the pond and locate where the big trout surface-feed. I took the binoculars into our bedroom. It was dark outside, but the lights were on inside Lodge One. They sat on the divan in the main room, alternately drinking and kissing. When they entered the front bedroom, I gave them five minutes. Werner snored, one of his habits. I walked the dam in sneakers and paused near their front bedroom. They were in bed, only a few feet distant from where I stood. Shellenbach scored that first night. Captain, are you interested?"

"I'm breathless."

"The next days began to follow the pattern established on Monday. They became inseparable. They fished from the dam or a boat. They went for walks in the woods. She swam near the spillway and he watched. At six o'clock they were together in Lodge Twelve and I presume they had cocktails and a meal. Afterward they returned to Lodge One for the evening. Also, I no longer snooped. Captain, is there a possibility that Shellenbach used a listening device against us?"

"That is usually one of their illegal dirty tricks."

"Oh, he is a fink!"

There was a long pause.

"Captain, I'd better round this off. I'm guessing Noornan has a tendency toward Lesbianism. I've met Lesbians and been propositioned by them. They have their little telltale gestures, can't keep their hands off you, and—skip it! It's an opinion, but based on fact. However, here are facts. Noornan was in total control of Shellenbach. She always led and he trailed along. She liked to make strong gestures. She'd say something and point. He would jump into action, like moving a porch chair a few inches. Lastly, I'd say that Noornan was always in full control of her emotions and her actions were determined by a keen mind, perhaps even a calculating mind. Her motivation would be whatever was best for Noornan. With a sucker like Shellenbach, her motivation would be whatever she had uppermost in her mind when she first stalked him on Monday afternoon. He played her game, whatever it was and wherever it led him, urged on by sex. Captain, you better wake up."

Raber opened his eyes.

"You," he said approvingly, "would make a good detective."

"I leave that job to you."

She rose gracefully and Raber stood.

"Captain, my well on Noornan is dry."

"Thank you very much."

"Damn it, I like you!"

"My dear, the feeling is mutual."

"Are you happily married?"

"Yes."

"You have children?"

"A four-year-old daughter and and a three-year-old son."

"You're a lucky man."

They shook hands warmly.

"Captain, now may I speak my piece?"

"Of course."

"If you arrive at the conclusion that somebody did drown Shellenbach in that pond, you can eliminate Werner as a suspect. You see, he has no motive. What about Evelyn Noornan? She is much stronger than that physical weakling. Suppose that late on Friday night, inside Lodge One, they had some strong disagreement? Maybe he stepped out of line. Maybe they struggled. He fell and hit his head on—skip that! Captain, why didn't you probe into *my* background?"

"Your personal life is none of my business."

"I'll tell the story anyway. Before my marriage, I was an airline hostess. When my husband disappeared with every dime we owned, including a hefty joint bank account and two cars, I was jobless and broke and bitter. I knew a former pilot who retired early and handled a stable of professionals. He signed me on. In June, my assignment was a Werner DeHaven at Twin Springs Trout Club and I drove there. One night became three nights. In mid-July I accompanied him on a long business trip. Do you mind a continuation?"

"Not at all."

"We've been together since then and in this apartment I'm a kept woman. We're good for each other. He had the quaint idea if he paid for sex he received full value in return, but I taught him to forget selfishness and consider the woman. We complement each other and since meeting him I haven't slept with anyone else."

She smiled suddenly.

"After his divorce we're going to be married. Surprised?"

"Not at all. He's a lucky man."

"While he was still a bricklayer," she mused, "Werner married. He scaled the success ladder, but she only made it up the first rung. There are no children. She began to drink and is now an alcoholic who hasn't left the house in months. Werner has tried to help her and has spent a fortune on psychiatrists, cure centers, the works, even hypnosis. At the trout club, captain, you think Shellenbach was after divorce evidence?"

"Yes."

"Forget that angle. Werner is a normal man with a strong

sex appetite. In his position at the top of the ladder he deserves a woman who can go wherever he goes. Doctors have advised that his wife has at the most a few months to live. She's in a rest home with round-the-clock attention. Werner's lawyers have filed for a divorce and that is why he'd never have drowned Shellenbach."

She turned Raber around and gave him a little push.
"Please leave, I'm about to cry!"
He left promptly.

6

FRED RABER entered an office building at 1326 McCarter Boulevard, glanced at a wall directory, and climbed the stairs to the second floor where the name OLIVER ASSOCIATES, INC., decorated a pebbled-glass door. In a receptionist's office an elderly man sat behind a desk with a nameplate identifying him as Mr. Hayes.

"Can I help you?" Hayes asked.

"I'm expected. Captain Fred Raber."

"And you are *late* for a ten thirty appointment."

"Sorry."

"No one is permitted to be late with Mr. Oliver."

"He must be a very fortunate man."

"And very important. Where is Fair Hills?"

"Route Seventeen, near the New York State border at Suffern. Aren't you further delaying the appointment?" Raber suggested.

Hayes spoke into an intercom: "Your pleasure, Mr. Oliver? Thank you, sir. Mr. Oliver decided to overlook tardiness," Hayes told Raber. "*That* door. Last office, left off the hallway."

That door opened on a central hallway, small offices on the left. Midway to the rear, on the right, Raber glanced through an open door. Two men sat at desks, their backs to the hallway, and there were six unoccupied desks. He continued to a left door marked PRESIDENT, knocked, and entered.

In a tastefully furnished master office, with subdued lighting, floor-to-ceiling drapes provided the background for a massive desk. The man who presided behind it wore his long black hair parted on the left side. His face was tanned, the lips a thin line, and the dark eyes expressionless, like those of a toad. He wore a tailored jacket in light gray, a blue knitted shirt with a yellow necktie, and a white display handkerchief. The desk hid the rest of his clothes.

"I'm Gardner Oliver," he announced, gesturing Raber into a chair. "You are late and I am a busy executive. How old are you?"

"I'm thirty-four," Raber said as he sat down.

"That is rather an immature age for a police captaincy."

Oliver leaned back, preparatory to dropping more pearls.

"At age twenty-seven I was on this city's police force, studying the rungs of the ladder up ahead. I might have become a captain at age forty-five." For a moment, he inventoried the manicured nails of his left hand. "I resigned from the force. Today I am president and sole owner of the largest private detective agency in Newark. Your telephoned message was unusual and also cryptic. Why?"

"That often happens when a message is conveyed secondhand."

"What is your reason for this meeting?"

"You employ a detective, Harry Shellenbach?"

Oliver nodded.

"How long has he been in your employ?"

"For nine years, Raber. How long have you been employed by the Fair Hills Police Department?"

"For four years. Shellenbach was staying at the Twin Springs Trout Club, in my town, for one week?"

"I believe so. What is the size of your force?"

"It's small, only twenty-two officers. Was Shellenbach working on a case for you at Twin Springs?"

"Absolutely not. He was on a vacation. What's the size of your town?"

"We are small, seventeen thousand. The weekly cost at the trout club is two hundred fifty dollars. Isn't that rather steep for Shellenbach?"

"No, Harry is my top man and I pay him handsomely. What is your salary scale at Fair Hills?"

"It's adequate. Is Shellenbach a good fisherman?"

"I rate him good. How long have you been a captain?"

"For three months. While your top detective vacationed, did he have occasion to phone you?"

"Ummm, I believe he phoned once. Why do you ask?"

"Mr. Oliver, do you remember his reason?"

"Frankly, I receive many, many important phone calls every day. Harry phoned on Thursday or possibly yesterday. As I remember, we talked briefly, a very casual talk. He thanked me for the loan of a fishing rod."

"Was his vacation proceeding satisfactorily?"

Oliver leaned forward. "I believe so. What is so urgent that you had to come here?"

The sparring had ended as Raber reported, "I met your top detective this morning. At seven A.M. out at Twin Springs. He wore red swim trunks. He was in the pond. He had drowned."

Oliver shot up from his chair with a startled "My God!" He sank back slowly. "That's unbelievable! I don't get it." He leaned forward tensely. "Like that, drowned! Is there an explanation?"

"Frankly, we don't know. That is why I drove here promptly. Was Shellenbach on a case for you?"

"Positively not!"

"What were his drinking habits?"

"That is unimportant. Captain, what facts are you withholding?"

"Mr. Oliver, I'm leveling with you and I expect you to level with me. Last night was warm and the windows were open at the other lodges. Not a single guest heard any unusual sounds. Shellenbach was last seen at eight o'clock. What were his drinking habits?"

"He was a one-martini man. My men are all temperate."

"How good a swimmer was he?"

Oliver brushed the question aside by saying, "All fishermen can swim and at times have to. Captain Raber, I am familiar with police tactics. What facts are you withholding?"

"Nothing. I came here in good faith to secure any information about Shellenbach that might explain the drowning. I'd like facts on his medical history. Was he subject to heart attacks? Or diabetic shocks? Or frequent dizzy spells?"

"No," Oliver answered carefully. "For your information,

my doctors run a complete physical check on each of my men every year. He always gave Harry a clean bill of health."

"How many operatives do you have?"

"We're big. I have a dozen regulars and fifteen to twenty part-timers. I hire unlimited extras for the biggest jobs." Oliver stared at Raber. "You have no explanation whatsoever for the drowning?"

"No, but there is this possibility. The lodge where he stayed almost abuts the pond, the dam is rather narrow, and the water is fifteen feet deep. Shellenbach may have slipped and fallen in."

"Not Harry, he's the last word in caution!"

"Perhaps he overate and swam too soon afterward."

"Harry never was a glutton!"

"Would he be inclined to swim alone at night?"

"That I doubt, but he could swim."

Raber thought for a moment. "We're exhausting the possibilities that might cause a drowning or contribute to it. What was your top operative's attitude toward women?"

"I fail to see—"

Oliver paused. Then he laughed contemptuously.

"Are there females around a trout club? I do a lot of fishing, and am considered to be an expert, and I've met females who fish! Believe me, most of them should be cut up and used as bait. What's this about Harry and women?"

"Let me phrase the problem like this," Raber suggested. "You knew him intimately for nine years. I only know the physical layout at Twin Springs. What I need from you is information that places Shellenbach in proper perspective against that background. What was his attitude toward women?"

"Harry had been divorced for years," Oliver answered. "Now she's married and Harry has been out of touch with her. Women, eh? Harry did have a saying about them. Something like, 'If it's handed to me, I won't toss it over my shoulder.'" Oliver gestured impatiently. "Hell, I'll be very frank with you, captain. I doubt that females would have found Harry very attractive."

"Thanks for your help, Mr. Oliver. There is one final

problem. We need a positive identification of the corpse. Did Shellenbach have any relatives in this area?"

"I believe they are mostly in the Chicago area where Harry was born. I think there's a Jersey cousin, but I have no idea where."

"Mr. Oliver, I know you're a very busy man, but this is an urgent problem. If your car is handy, I can lead the way to the county morgue at Ardnor. You can be back here in less than two hours." Raber smiled. "For Harry?"

"Of course."

They rose, and Oliver added, "I'll rearrange my appointment list and make a phone call."

"That's very generous of you. I'll telephone the county authorities to let them know we're on the way."

"Please use the phone in the receptionist's office. Tell Hayes the call is on the house."

7

AT THE morgue in the basement of Telford County's administration building in Ardnor, the county seat, two officials waited—Major John Orwell, who headed the county's investigative staff, and George Freund, a morgue official. Raber introduced Gardner Oliver. Preceded by Freund, Oliver left the room.

"Freddy," Orwell said heartily, "I didn't expect to see you today. Are you an ESP expert?"

"No, major."

"Then you must be prescient. How the hell did you know that Harry Shellenbach had been murdered?"

"I know because you just told me. We're pressed for time. Oliver failed to level with me in Newark and that's why I wanted him here in our jurisdiction to make the identification. Can you skim the facts for me?"

"Dr. Wightman found no external signs of violence on the corpse," Orwell said rapidly. "He siphoned a water sample from the lungs and ran a cursory test that proved the water was pure and hard. He had procured a sample of pond water and knew this would test out relatively soft and also contain impurities, like tiny bits of decayed vegetable matter. He phoned me and I came right over. Right now we have a lab technician conducting comparison tests on the water samples. What is your guess as to the probable source of hard water?"

"I'll bet it's artesian supplied to Twin Springs by our Water Department. If I'm right, the technician should find a small amount of chlorine." Raber drew out his wallet. "I have here—"

A door opened. Oliver and Freund returned.

"Yes?" Raber prompted politely.

"I'm sorry to say the corpse is Harry Shellenbach." Oliver shivered. "It's cold in there."

Freund said casually, "It has to be," and sat at his desk.

"Mr. Oliver," Orwell went on cordially, "we appreciate your help in driving here from Newark. Now our assistant medical examiner can proceed with the autopsy."

"Will this be a complete autopsy?" Oliver asked.

"Well, he'll start with an analysis of the contents of the stomach and the digestive tract. Last night, about eight o'clock, the victim dined on a broiled trout. That should give us a good idea of the approximate time he drowned."

"Major," Oliver purred, "doesn't such an analysis often prove to be inaccurate by an hour or two?"

"So the ME keeps warning me." Orwell smiled affably. "Would you join Mr. Freund and complete our records?"

Oliver sat at the desk.

Orwell winked at Oliver's back and asked, "Freddy, did you bring that affidavit I need in the Ackerson case?"

"Yes, I did." For a second time Raber produced his wallet. He withdrew a form and he opened it for the major's inspection. "That's the basis for the data." He pointed to the printed heading: *Water Department, Borough of Fair Hills.* "This was completed yesterday." He indicated more lettering: *Daily Analysis, Artesian Well Water, 7 September.* "Note certain hard facts, major." Raber fingered certain percentages of mineral content such as iron, calcium, and chlorine, the last an additive as an insurance against any contamination. "Doesn't it look like the Ackerson case has become technical?"

"I'll send this form right up to the lab," Orwell decided. "George, give me a spare envelope."

Freund produced the item and handed it to Orwell, who sealed the form inside the envelope. Using a wall surface for support, he printed on the envelope:

FOR: DR. WIGHTMAN, URGENT
FROM: CAPTAIN FRED RABER

He added the word THOROUGHNESS and underlined it.

"Did you find him a bit upset?" Raber murmured.

"Of course he was upset. Sometimes I think certain policemen need a guide to find the john."

With the paperwork completed at the desk, Orwell gave the envelope to Freund with instructions to deliver it immediately and Freund left.

"Mr. Oliver, we'll adjourn to my office for a quick summary."

They rode an elevator to the fourth floor. In an anteroom an officer monitored a battery of telephones and a shortwave system. In an office next door, Orwell gestured Raber and Oliver to seats on opposite sides of a central desk. He closed the door and remained standing, one elbow propped atop a filing cabinet. The three men formed a triangle, with Oliver between Raber and Orwell.

"Freddy," Orwell suggested, "let me hear the background."

Raber filled in the details, then suggested to Oliver that for the major's benefit they should review their conversation earlier that morning in Oliver's office in Newark.

"While a guest at Trout Springs, Harry Shellenbach worked on a case for your firm?" Raber asked.

"Absolutely not," Oliver said promptly.

"The victim had an excellent medical history, checked every year by your personal doctor?"

"Correct, captain."

"No heart trouble, diabetes, dizzy spells, or such?"

"Correct."

"Victim a moderate drinker?"

"Assuredly."

"I believe you said a one-martini man?"

"Yes."

"Inclined to eat heavily?"

"No."

"Proficiency as a swimmer?"

"Reasonable."

"Proficiency as a fisherman?"

"Good."

"Two hundred fifty dollars—the cost of a week's vacation

at Trout Springs. This posed no financial stress for the victim?"

"None whatsoever. Harry Shellenbach was highly paid, as I hope you two officers are."

"Thank you," Orwell said.

"I believe we also established," Raber continued, "that the victim phoned you on the morning of Thursday, September sixth?"

"Correct, but only for a moment or two."

"Casual call, I believe you said. The victim was enjoying his vacation and thanked you for the loan of a fishing rod."

"Yes."

"During our conversation, Mr. Oliver, you said the victim was not particularly attractive to women?"

"Harsh words, captain, but substantially correct."

"Therefore, the victim was not a chaser?"

"Not Harry."

"And at all times the victim was a careful cautious man who would not fall into the pond by accident, eh?"

"Yes."

"Thank you very much, Mr. Oliver, for your patience." Raber turned to Orwell. "Rather sketchy, major, but that's what we have for the background. Wait—one more item." Raber turned to Oliver. "Against the information you supplied in Newark, sir, how do you explain that last night, at Twin Springs Trout Club, in Fair Hills, my jurisdiction, your top operative, Harry Shellenbach, was murdered?"

An electric shock coursed through Oliver.

"You didn't tell me that in Newark!" he exploded.

"I just learned that fact from Major Orwell."

"But—but—"

"Mr. Oliver, this morning in Newark, I leveled with you. Why did you lie to me?"

"I did not!"

"Mr. Oliver, listen very carefully. You are now in *our* jurisdiction. I inform you that you are about to be interrogated as a witness in a first-degree murder case, about which you have pertinent information. As a citizen, you are expected to cooperate. Also, to answer any and all questions fully and truthfully. If you wish you may choose to remain silent. If you wish the services of a lawyer, you may make one phone call. Clear, Mr. Oliver?"

"I have nothing to hide!"

"Do you wish the services of a lawyer?"

"Absolutely not!"

"When I questioned you in Newark, why did you lie?"

"I—did—not—lie!"

"Ah, you told me the victim, while at Twin Springs, was not working on a case for your firm."

"That's the truth, Raber."

"You take some advice from me," Orwell drawled from his vantage point by the filing cabinet. "In the State of New Jersey you are a registered private investigator with a substantial bond posted in your behalf. You are expected to cooperate with the police, particularly during a first-degree murder investigation. Otherwise that bond is subject to forfeit and you may lose your license to operate. A final point, Mr. Oliver. This is no mystery program on TV where a private detective always stands up successfully to the police. You try that role and I'll go after your scalp. I repeat this question: While he stayed at Twin Springs Trout Club, Harry Shellenbach worked on a case for your firm?"

For the first time Oliver hesitated.

"My, my," Raber chided politely, "this poor man needs assistance in answering a simple question. Let us approach the matter of his veracity from another angle. Are you acquainted with a certain Mrs. Werner DeHaven?"

"Yes," Oliver admitted.

"That's better. Did Mrs. DeHaven employ your firm to obtain evidence for a divorce against her husband, a wealthy building contractor, business address, Plank Road, Newark?"

"Yes," Oliver mumbled.

"During this week, with the victim in residence at Lodge One, you *knew* Werner DeHaven vacationed at nearby Lodge Two?"

"Yes."

"Thank you, sir. It was Mrs. DeHaven who approached

you on the matter of securing evidence in a divorce from her husband?"

"She did."

"She visited your office, 1326 McCarter Boulevard, Newark?"

"Yes."

"At that time Mrs. DeHaven was alone?"

"For God's sake, Raber, wives who are being deceived by their husbands are often alone when they seek out my services!"

"Then answer yes to the question. When did Mrs. DeHaven, alone, consult you at your office?"

"In July." Oliver gestured impatiently. "I cannot specify the exact day without consulting our office records."

"Quite understandable, sir." Raber smiled politely. "From here on I see no point in your remaining evasive. Particularly since it should be apparent I already have the factual answer to any question I intend to ask. For example: isn't the corespondent a Mrs. Jayne L. Lorning, Apartment 1418, B-Complex, Highline Apartments, Addison Street, Newark, New Jersey?"

"Yes."

"And Mrs. Lorning was in residence with Werner DeHaven, Lodge Two, Twin Springs, this past week?"

"Yes."

"So that it was your firm, sir, not the victim, who actually paid the two-hundred-fifty-dollar fee for a one week's stay at Lodge One?"

"All right."

"Mr. Oliver, one other angle."

Raber rose to stare down at Oliver.

"We return to Thursday morning, September sixth. At that time the victim talked to you over the telephone?"

"And I said it was a casual call, only a minute or—"

"Stop the nonsense," Raber interrupted coldly. "The victim phoned you at nine fifteen A.M., from an outside phone booth, located in West Shopping Center, off Broad Street, in Fair Hills. Also, the victim read to the operator the number on his Bell Telephone credit card."

Raber turned to Orwell.

"Major, here is the president of the largest private detective agency in Newark who wants us to believe Bell Tel keeps no records of charged calls. Bell Tel timed the length of that call. Our detective who was tailing the victim at the time also timed that call. That call took over five minutes and it was no casual call."

Raber returned to Oliver, who was sweating.

"Do you wish the services of a lawyer?"

"I have nothing to hide."

"Then start telling the truth. What was the subject matter of that phone call?"

Oliver took a deep breath.

"We had planned to raid the premises of Lodge Two. We had already set the date for Saturday night and—uh, that would have been tonight. We were to go in at nine o'clock to firm the divorce evidence with pictures and witnesses. Harry insisted we cancel the raid."

"Why?"

"He explained that the front entrance was trapped at night with a photoelectric eye. When our car entered with the raiding party, a bell would ring a warning in the club's office. Management would investigate promptly and they have three or four tough employees always around. They'd catch us trespassing on private property. Harry insisted they'd smash our expensive cameras and kick our asses off the premises. So I called off the raid."

"What else did the victim tell you?"

"Nothing."

"What equipment, owned by the firm, did the victim take with him on this case?"

"Binoculars and a Leica camera."

Raber waited. Oliver sat silent. Orwell picked up the cue.

"Come off it, Mr. Oliver. You were not asked *what equipment* unless we already knew the answer. What type listening device?"

"Very expensive, Japanese make." Oliver shrugged. "It cost twelve hundred dollars. I—I—well, I'd like it returned. If possible, major?"

Orwell countered: "Big Ear?"

"We call it that—uh, in the trade."

"Illegal, too, isn't it?"

Oliver shrugged.

"Earlier this morning in your office," Raber continued, "it occurred to you we had made a very fast make on the victim?"

"It did."

"And on you?"

"Yes."

"And on your address?"

"Well, you said Harry had drowned. Naturally I assumed you had inspected Harry's wallet and—"

"I have yet to see Harry's wallet," Raber interrupted. "This is not a fishing expedition, no pun intended. We not only made the victim on Thursday morning, September sixth, we also made you. Exactly what kind of flimsy cover do you maintain to protect the identity of an operative working on a case?"

Raber paused to let that soak in.

"Routinely, we broke that cover in minutes. The victim's phone call to you on Thursday morning. The victim said he was involved in something else at Twin Springs?"

"No."

"*Not* the divorce case. Another, *big* matter?"

"No."

"Perhaps a lot of loose cash lying around—blackmail?"

"Harry would never—" Oliver glanced up sharply. "Captain, I have no idea what's in your mind. Harry was honest. He talked only about the pending divorce case."

"The victim told you he had just visited the Fair Hills HQ?"

"No."

"Hiding his identity, trying to pump us?"

"No!"

"Of course he didn't. That's why we suspected he was involved in some deep trouble out there. That's why we broke his cover. Frankly, we thought him a poor excuse for a private investigator. Frankly, he might be alive today if he had had the common sense to level with us and not play silly games. And I'll bet the victim didn't tell you he drank heavily at Twin Springs, a minimum of one quart of hard stuff per day?"

"My God, no!"

"Or that he was involved, sexually, with a very attractive brunette who is an expert fisherman?"

"No!"

"Isn't it a fact that the victim was a lousy fisherman?"

"Well—"

Raber decided Oliver had it coming to him and delivered the first blast.

"It seems, Mr. Oliver, that while your top operative was on a case a lot transpired about which you knew absolutely nothing. So much, as a matter of record, that he became the victim of a first-degree murder."

Raber turned to Orwell.

"I'm convinced, major, this dummy knows nothing that will aid us in this murder case."

"Agreed," Orwell drawled. "Mr. Oliver, thank you very much for coming here and identifying the body of your top operative. Even you couldn't bungle that assignment. I suggest you keep this point in mind for future guidance: If you or one of your representatives with illegal listening devices ever visit this county again and put on a questionable performance, believe me, I'll go after licenses. You are dismissed, Mr. Oliver."

Oliver rose to leave. Raber's voice jerked him to a stop short of the closed door.

"Oliver!"

Slowly the man turned.

Raber readied a final blast.

"Not only did you prove yourself a rotten liar, but you are also a rotten bastard."

"Nobody talks to me like that!" Oliver flared.

"Why don't you sue me? I repeat, sue me, you rotten bastard. Major Orwell can be your witness and so will I. You *know* Mrs. Werner DeHaven never visited your office on a divorce matter in July. Or visited your office at any other time. Oliver, there are two types of private investigative agencies. The first works hard and honestly and efficiently to establish a solid reputation in the community. That takes time, but brings a line of steady customers to the door. You belong to the second type, fortunately a minority. You shot up the ladder too fast. You didn't wait for clients to arrive. You went out and made business, every dirty dollar you could produce, precisely as you did with Mrs. DeHaven."

Raber wheeled to Orwell.

"This rotten bastard knew Mrs. DeHaven was an incurable alcoholic with a few months to live. He knew she had not been out of her home, alone, for months. He knew DeHaven was wealthy and had another woman. So he went to Mrs. DeHaven's home with the news and procured her signature on a contract to obtain divorce evidence. Major, can I spit on this scum?"

"Too late, he just scooted off," Orwell advised.

"Freddy, this is the first time I ever heard you swear. Relax on your day off. Did he supply any help?"

"Here and there," Raber answered, starting to calm down. "I didn't know that Shellenbach had a Big Ear on the job or that the employees have the front entrance trapped at night. The victim may have been unattractive to females, but I understand that the woman he became involved with was a luscious doll."

"Could a segment of the club's management be the killers?"

"It has to be them, but I haven't the slightest idea how to tie them into the killing."

"What light did this doll shed on the matter?"

"She drove home from the club last night and we haven't caught up with her yet. May I ask a favor?"

Orwell patted Raber's slim shoulder.

"Will I sit on this murder, eh? We owe you, Freddy. In February you bailed us out of that mess in Cumberland Township. You can have my right arm and any manpower you need. But stay relaxed and keep an objective approach. Also, no more careless words like 'thoroughness.' If reporters ask, this murder is an accident. . . . That's better, Freddy, you're smiling."

They shook hands.

8

ALONGSIDE A small table on the porch at Lodge Two, Werner DeHaven sat with a tall, frosted glass at his elbow. Raber remained standing and handed him a typed deposition.

He explained, "This is the final step in the routine for you," and smiled. "I'd like you to check the story you told me for accuracy."

DeHaven read a few sentences, glanced up sharply.

"For crissakes, Raber!" he protested. "This story makes me sound like a sixth grader!"

"Not true," Raber said mildly, with no intention of dropping the Hicksville mask. "You told your story like I was a sixth grader. Is your story accurate?"

DeHaven finished reading the deposition and nodded agreement. Raber handed him a ball-point pen and DeHaven signed his name. Raber added the time, two thirty P.M., and the date, September 8, and signed as a witness, but did not add his title.

"Thank you, Mr. DeHaven, for your help. The drowning is all wrapped up. It was accidental."

"I don't agree with your conclusion, Raber."

"Is something bothering you?"

"Damned right there is! I'm not a cop, but if I was, I wouldn't label the drowning an accident."

"I don't tell you how to run your business, Mr. DeHaven. You want to tell me how to run my job?"

"For five days," DeHaven growled, "Shellenbach always wore red swim trunks around the pond, but nobody ever saw him in the water. Doesn't that seem odd to you?"

"Maybe."

"And he drowned at night! Isn't that also odd?"

"If a man wants to swim or not swim, that's his decision and that goes for swimming at night."

"You questioned Evelyn Noornan?" DeHaven demanded.

"No, she drove home last night."

"You intend to question her?"

"What for?"

"I'll tell you what for Sherlock!"

DeHaven began to punctuate each sentence by stabbing a forefinger at Raber.

"An accidental drowning stinks! In a bikini, Noornan was very attractive! They were always together and she's very strong and Shellenbach is a weak fish! Last night inside Lodge One he went for her! She knocked him down and he smacked his head against a hard object, understand? Noornan checked him and he's dead! Sure, it's an accident, but she panicked. She lugged the body outside and eased it into the pond. That was to make it look like an accidental drowning and fool the stupid police. She drove home to—well, set up an alibi. Am I getting through to you, Sherlock?"

"I think you watch too many mysteries on TV," Raber remarked calmly. "I saw one once where a man got killed and he was just knocked down and hit his head on a rug."

Raber started off, turned slowly.

"Mr. DeHaven, do you know Newark?"

"That's an excellent deduction, Sherlock."

"So you do know Newark?"

"I lived there all my life."

"Maybe you can help me on another matter."

"Are you hinting you have two problems with which you cannot cope?"

"Guess—so. Met a fellow, said he worked for the biggest private detective agency in Newark. Any idea what one?"

"Oliver Associates," DeHaven said softly.

"That's it," Raber agreed. "This fellow give me a hard time, treated me like I was a dummy. You know this Oliver, maybe?"

"I know Gardner Oliver."

"What's he like?"

For a moment, DeHaven sat silent, his face inscrutable, his

big hands clenching and unclenching. He stared across the pond, then began to talk, more to the water than to Raber.

"I had a wildcat strike on a building complex. On the second night a valuable piece of equipment was doused with gasoline and fired. The next day I received a phone call from Oliver, who said he had heard about my trouble on a radio broadcast. He offered to supply private guards, around the clock, to prevent a recurrence. I hedged, then drove to the site, where I talked to union delegates and pickets. Some of those men had been my close friends in the old days. They denied sabotage. I told them about the phone call from Oliver. A union rep told about a similar deal involving Oliver and another contractor. The workers volunteered to guard the site at night and they did. I phoned Oliver the news. No more sabotage and the strike ended three days later."

"Hey, sounds like this Oliver fired your equipment!"

"Sherlock, you bite right through to the bone."

"This Oliver *makes* business, right?"

"That's his reputation in Newark."

Raber strolled across the dam and entered Lodge One.

"Pal!" he shouted. "Time to wake up!"

Responding to the cue, Boyce said loudly, "Just dozed off. We through wastin' time here?"

"Yeah, all wrapped up. The guy drowned by accident. You got his duds in his car?"

"Hours ago, pal."

Under the cathedral ceiling of the main room of Lodge One, at a center table, Raber produced a ball-point and a notebook. Urgently, Boyce pointed in the direction of the nearby barn. He cupped his hands to his eyes, indicating somebody in the upstairs apartment there had been watching Lodge One with binoculars. Raber pantomimed that somebody might be monitoring them with a listening device. Now, understanding each other, Raber scrawled a terse message: *M-1. Not pond water in H. S.'s lungs. FHWD's water.*

Boyce nodded, then asked loudly, "You hungry?"

"Nothing to eat since early breakfast."

"I'll fix you a sandwich in the kitchen."

Boyce beckoned, leading the way into the lavatory.

He switched on a light to disclose an old-fashioned tub set on metal paws, a shower curtain drawn back even with a spray head. Boyce faked stoppering the drain and turning on the cold-water tap. Next, he hoisted an imaginary body into the tub and held an imaginary head under the water, indicating a high ring inside the tub. This was followed by letting the water drain from the tub. He laid an imaginary body atop a mat he took from the tub's edge. From a rack he handed Raber a large towel. The towel was still damp and heavily smudged with black marks, like dust. Boyce pantomimed that this towel had been used to dry a body and wipe surplus water off the linoleum. He pointed under the near edge of the tub, elevated four inches above the linoleum. Raber dropped to his knees to peer under the tub. Evidently, last night, the killer or killers had erred. Under the tub, missed by whoever had used the towel as a mop, were four small pools of water that could have dripped from the wet corpse. Raber rose. Carefully, Boyce placed the items in their former positions and the two returned to the main room.

The MO was partially clear.

However, how had the killer or killers managed to overpower the victim without the man making an outcry?

He had been taken unaware, of course, a swift and deadly attack to render the victim unconscious. Subsequent to the drowning in the tub, the corpse had been slid quietly into the pond.

"Pal, how's that sandwich?" Boyce asked loudly.

Raber answered, "So far so good," and wrote in the notebook: *One Leica camera?*

Boyce nodded.

Raber added: *One pair binoculars?*

Again, Boyce nodded.

"Good sandwich," Raber said, and wrote: *Listening device. Trade name Big Ear?*

Boyce shook his head. Taking the ball-point, he wrote

swiftly: *Wallet missing. Searched every square foot. 20 minutes. Located, bottom laundry bag, front bedroom. Positive, no Big Ear inside lodge.* He eyed Raber.

Raber wrote: *They have it?*

Boyce shrugged.

Raber wrote: *Hidden outside?*

Again Boyce shrugged.

Raber said, "I'll call a squad car so we can get outa here," and pocketed the ball-point and notebook.

They went outside where the sloped roof extended partly over the wide porch. Raber headed for his unmarked car, raised Officer Nosse on shortwave, and issued orders.

"Send Kelly to Twin Springs in a squad car. Have him pick up Sergeant Parisi, who is on foot patrol in the business district. Parisi is to drive the victim's Mustang to headquarters. Tell Kelly to hit the siren on Haycock Road to alert us. Out."

Raber strolled toward Lodge One.

When you knew that Big Ear was not inside, and if it were still on the premises, it should be simple to locate it, he thought.

He paused and studied the outside of the lodge.

Four feet from the pond water, the porch rested on the ground, so it was not a possible cache. He leaned against a post that supported the porch's north end. Boyce sat nearby on a chair. The lodge's north end was a solid run down to the steps and afforded no hiding place. Raber assumed, also, that the south end duplicated the north side. And Shellenbach was a reasonably careful man, who had hidden his wallet in the bottom of a laundry bag. However, he would want Big Ear hidden close enough for quick and easy access. That ruled out the high rear end of the lodge, leaving only the roof's overhang.

"Who's gonna get into the World Series?" Raber asked Boyce.

Boyce began to kick the subject around. Casually, Raber studied the numerous spaces between the rafters of the roof that rested atop the plate rail of the front wall. Then he sat beside Boyce and wrote in his notebook: *You join the squad car when it arrives. Unlock the Mustang. Parisi drives it home. Then Kelly hits the siren hard.*

Boyce nodded in understanding and Raber pocketed the notebook.

"Old pal, we forgot something," Raber said.

"Forgot what?"

"Loot."

Raber entered the lodge. In the kitchen he located a large brown paper bag and took a full bottle of white wine from a shelf. Back on the porch, leaning against the post, in full view of the watcher in the barn's apartment, he displayed the wine bottle.

"I like wine," Boyce said and chuckled.

"Me, too."

Raber placed the bottle inside the bag and sat by Boyce where they chatted until a siren keened softly on Haycock Road. Boyce left. Behind Lodge One, voices sounded. A car door opened and slammed. An engine started up. Suddenly a siren began to wail. Instantly Raber was on his feet and active. As the siren ceased, he strolled to his car, carrying the paper sack, then drove slowly toward the farmhouse where a small parade formed.

In the lead, Kelly drove a blue-white squad car. Parisi followed at the wheel of the Mustang. Then, Boyce in his new Ford and Raber at the rear.

As he eased around the farmhouse, he saw Gene Palan standing by the office door. Palan posed immobile, arms folded across his chest, face stained red in anger. Raber stopped the car.

"Wrapped up," he said. "Your guest drowned, accident."

Palan glared.

As he drove off, Raber thought, And Hicksville wrapped up, too, I hope, and joined the end of the parade.

9

IT WAS late Saturday afternoon, September 8.

Inside police headquarters the door into Chief Hocking's office was closed and three officers were grouped at the desk—Raber, Boyce, and Lieutenant Sprague, who was in uniform.

"Until the chief returns home on Monday morning," Raber explained, "this is the way we play a first-degree murder. Presently, we have no plausible motive. We conceal the few cards we hold. Suspicion points directly at the Twin Springs employees. They have the means and the opportunity. Personally, I dislike secrecy, but we have no alternative. We convinced the employees we are dumb cops and that gives us a slight edge. The drowning remains an accident and Major Orwell will cooperate for a while. Right here, only we three know the drowning is a murder. Possibly Nosse and Montanez may suspect murder, but I doubt they'll gossip and I plan no gags for them. However, if anyone hears any talk about a possible murder, soft-pedal it, clear?"

Sprague said, "There's no advantage in tipping our hand," and Boyce added, "We are already working in the dark against the employees and that gives them a big advantage."

"Here's the groundwork for a report to the chief," Raber continued, "and it updates everybody. Roy, you learned from Gene Palan that Evelyn Noornan lives in an apartment at London Terrace in New York City. What is his story for last night?"

"I'll skip his college vocabulary," Boyce said promptly. "He said he hit the sack at ten o'clock. A ringing phone awakened him. This originated from the office opposite the downstairs room where he lives. He answered the ringing phone at the switchboard and a man asked to be connected with Noornan in Lodge Twelve. The man gave no name and Palan saw no point in inquiring. Palan made the necessary connection, hung up the moment Noornan answered. He did note the time on the office's electric clock, twelve twenty A.M., and knew he might have trouble going back to sleep. So he went into the kitchen and heated a glass of milk and returned to the office. He saw the incoming call had been ended and disconnected the line to Lodge Twelve. Later, he heard the Corvette start up with a *VROOM*, Palan's word. When he heard the Corvette back out and start off, he thought Noornan might need some assistance and he stepped to the office porch where a night light was on. She spotted him and stopped. She said, now I quote Palan directly: 'I've been called to the city unexpectedly, and expect to return by Sunday.' Palan offered two unsolicited comments. He thought from her manner that she seemed upset and handled the Corvette inexpertly in driving through the entrance gate. And she turned right on Haycock Road and headed for town. Palan finished his milk and went to bed. He said he slept soundly until the chef roused him with the news that Shellenbach had drowned in the pond."

"Palan said 'city,' not 'New York City'?" Sprague asked.

"Yes."

"Not to her apartment or home?"

"No."

"You believe 'city' meant London Terrace?"

"I have no idea and thought it best not to ask."

Someone knocked on the door, and Raber said, "Come in."

Nosse stepped inside and closed the door.

"She made a phone call to Noornan's apartment earlier," Raber explained. "And received no answer. Any progress?"

"I just phoned a second time and heard the desk operator ringing. She told me 'no answer' and I took further action. Captain, I *did* do right?"

"I'm sure you did, but let's hear it."

"I asked the switchboard operator to connect me with the desk, and a man answered."

A smile flitted across her face.

"Captain, I've learned you are often devious in similar

situations. So I explained to this man that Miss Noornan and I worked for the same business organization, that I knew she was on vacation, but something important had come up. The matter needed her attention. I explained she had not answered her phone. Did he know of any way I might get in touch with her? He said to wait a moment. He came back on the line with the information their records showed she was still on vacation somewhere in New Jersey, but had not left the address. He also said her cotenant was in Maine. He added he had checked their joint mailbox and it was still full of mail. I thanked the man and closed the connection."

"It was wise, Nosse, not to give him a fake name, nor to ask questions about the cotenant. Today, no more phone calls to London Terrace. Tomorrow when you are on duty, in the morning, make a couple of calls. So, I'm devious, eh?"

Raber smiled.

"I can reach that address within an hour. I want to question Miss Noornan or her cotenant before either one realizes we are police and prepares a possible fabrication. You need a solid cover for the operator, the desk, or anyone home in the apartment." He thought a moment. "This should be safe. You are a reporter for the local *Clarion*, a weekly. You saw the guest list at Twin Springs, noticed the registration of a Miss Noornan. Female fisherman sounded like a good story, women's lib, etcetera. Work out the details. When you work the 'devious' angle, you need a plausible line of continuation, okay?" She nodded and left.

"She becomes a better officer every day," Sprague noted.

"Tell the chief," Raber suggested. "What's your report?"

"I had no time at Twin Springs to make notes," Sprague explained, "so this is off the top of my head. I played dumb for three hours and questioned the five employees casually. Nobody offered any new facts, but I had an opportunity to study each man. Here are my reactions and they're not colored by the fact that I now know Shellenbach was murdered. First: Diego Ramose, their chef. He's small, wiry, quick, and intelligent. He's a Puerto Rican in his early thirties. He's been in the States for seven years, is married, and has a four-year-old son. He likes to chatter and showed me the son's picture. In New York City he ran his own diner and it folded two years ago. He complained about poor help and long hours for himself. Next he held odd chef's jobs until April, this year, when he signed with Empire to come out here. He dislikes the country, but it's a steady job with top pay. I rate him the least-important employee. He might or might not stick a knife in somebody's ribs. He's a top chef." Sprague smiled. "What a breakfast he served me—I won't need to eat for two days. He delivered a broiled trout to Shellenbach at eight o'clock on Friday night. He knew the man had been drinking as there was an opened bottle of whiskey on the kitchen table and the man carried a half-filled glass. Ramose suggested wine with the trout and Shellenbach agreed. Second employee, a rung above Ramose: Joe Arragon. Hell, we all know he's a heavyweight in size. He does the menial chores like removing garbage and cleaning the lodges. Oh—Apex, in Suffern, supplies all the linens. Don't let his soft voice fool anybody, as he's quick and strong. He's probably a slow thinker and obeys orders. He could fold Shellenbach in two with one hand. Also, he moves around quietly like a big cat. Belatedly, I believe he might have done the job on Shellenbach, fast and quietly, with no questions asked. I rate him dangerous. Now we come to that sourball, Carl Krauthof, the copter pilot. He's in his early thirties, husky, and likes to brag. He flew choppers in Nam and we might check his military record. He's away a lot, ferrying guests and Paul Goodone on Empire's export-import business. The sour bastard dislikes any work assignments outside of flying. Fourth employee up the ladder: Gene Palan. I found him puzzling. He's obviously intelligent and well educated. Is Oppenheim, their lawyer in New York City, the real boss and Palan relays Oppenheim's orders to the others? Palan handles the arrival and departure of guests, does the billings, handles cash, and signs the paychecks. The chef told me that last item. He answers all correspondence and prefers the phone. Fred, he can't type. He's in his mid-fifties—courteous, pleasant, smooth. He has thick wrists and big-knuckled fingers and may be more powerful than he looks. Last employee: Paul Goodone. He's in his late thirties, I'd guess. He is solidly put together and weighs about a hundred eighty. He moves around—hell, like he had every step planned beforehand! His general attitude? You won't get any information out of me. I rate him the boss at Twin Springs." Sprague shrugged, then added quietly: "He always wears a deadpan face. In a gangster movie he'd play the role of a Mafia boss—tough, smart, amoral. Are there any questions on a particular employee or do you want the rest of it?"

"Good work," Raber approved. "What's the rest of it?"

"I'm a good friend of John Barrington and used to fish there for free. John gave me a tour of the farmhouse so I saw no point in checking upstairs with its six bedrooms, three used by Arragon, Krauthof, and Goodone. The chef bunks alone in the apartment in the barn. I didn't poke around the first floor where Palan lives, as I know the setup. I figured if anything is wrong out there it has to be in the basement. It's huge, the size of the farmhouse, and open except for stone pillars down the center. It's easily controlled because there are only two entrances. One is an outside hatch where the door can be bolted from the inside and the second entrance is the stairway off the kitchen. You bet I ate breakfast with my back next to that kitchen door! At eight o'clock the county parade arrived and the chef ran to a window. I suggested he go outside for a better view and he did. Palan hurried through the kitchen and went outside. Krauthof and Joe Arragon had already left the farmhouse. Goodone? I figured he was upstairs and hoped he stayed put. I opened the door into the basement and even at that point I wondered if the stairway was trapped. I went down only two steps and saw where they had built a new room, say ten feet by twenty feet, of solid boards and positioned alongside the front wall next to Haycock Road. That room had one door with—"

"Two padlocks," Raber interposed.

"Right," Sprague agreed, and eyed Raber thoughtfully. "Maybe that new room is the key to any illegality that led to Shellenbach's murder. And no employee knows I had a peek at the basement."

Boyce prompted: "Any more detail about the padlocks?"

"One is positioned above the doorknob and the other one below. The top one is black and the bottom one gold-colored."

"That suggests," Boyce reasoned, "that two different keys are needed to enter that room. If a different employee is in charge of a key, then both employees must be present before the room can be entered."

"Possibly," Sprague said. "The two padlocks might be there so that any outsider who wanted to break in would have a bigger problem."

Stepping in, Raber observed: "This is pure conjecture. We know management issues four bottles of liquor to each arriving guest. They must buy in wholesale lots, store the cases down there, and two padlocks could be precaution."

"Fred," Sprague objected, "opposite where I sat in the kitchen were two large closets with the doors open. In one closet liquor cases were stacked floor to ceiling."

"I fell on my face," Raber said. "What's next?"

Boyce pointed to a brown paper bag atop the desk.

"You're holding out on us," he chided. "I saw you put one bottle of wine in the bag, but it holds more now. And behind Lodge One, why did you have Kelly hit the siren hard except to draw the attention of the employees while you worked some ploy?"

"One piece of equipment was missing," Raber explained, "that Shellenbach had on the job. Either an employee had walked off with Big Ear or it had to be hidden outside because you didn't find it inside the lodge. I spotted something between two rafters atop the plate rail."

He opened the bag and set a bottle of unopened wine on the desk. Next he withdrew a single earphone attached to a cord with a plug on the opposite end.

"I spotted the arched metal."

He withdrew a rectangular box.

"One listening device, called Big Ear in the trade. Gardner Oliver wants it back and said it cost twelve hundred dollars. Probably Shellenbach used this illegal device to monitor conversation in Lodge Two."

"Care if I check it out?" Boyce asked.

"You're our gadget expert."

"It has an inside antenna," Boyce muttered, handling the box. "It's powered by transistor batteries. It's a Japanese model and Gardner Oliver one velly big liar. It sells for around four hundred dollars."

Boyce tried on the earphone, adjusting the receiver over his left ear.

"Good idea. My left ear hears outside reception and my right ear is free to hear local sounds."

He plugged in the cord and flicked on a switch.

"I'll give it a whirl for sensitivity."

He aimed the box toward the main building.

"Gentlemen, is the mayor working at his desk?"

A minute drifted past.

"Dick, what gives next door?"

"Tonight in the recreation hall the Junior League holds a dance. A lot of females are at work."

"Yes, and several are next door in the john powdering their noses. One told a dirty joke." Raber took off the earphone and grinned. "Is it time for a theory, Fred?"

"Go right ahead."

"I'd say this gadget is highly sensitive, say up to two hundred feet." Boyce clicked off the switch and aimed the box at Raber. "I'm Shellenbach beaming in on the quarry in Lodge Two. What time do they hit the sack? Do they sleep together? Do they sleep in the raw? How much sex? What's the best time to raid?"

Boyce yawned.

"Dullsville in Lodge Two. We know Gardner Oliver makes business. Maybe Shellenbach picks up and feeds him tips. Blackmail might be down their alley and it might be part of the racket at Twin Springs." Boyce aimed the box more to his right. "I'm beamed on Lodge Three." He paused. "A call girl is there with a wealthy guest. It's easy to obtain his name and address from his license plates and hit him later for a bundle of money. Fred, does this sound plausible?"

Raber nodded.

"Lodge Twelve," Boyce went on, "would be within range of Big Ear and Evelyn Noornan, who I hear is really stacked.

Too bad this gadget isn't closed-circuit TV!" He began to swivel the box to his left. "Theoretically, I'm now beaming north along Haycroft Road. Hey, I hear new voices coming in strong!"

Boyce snapped his fingers.

"Fred, if we kick this puzzle around long enough, maybe we can break it wide open. Suppose Shellenbach picked up Gene Palan and Paul Goodone talking about some illegal business? It involves money big enough to warrant murder. Anyway, my theory is Shellenbach played around with Big Ear and tumbled to some illegality at Twin Springs."

"Or he beamed into the farmhouse on purpose," Raber offered, "because he was an eager employee on the alert for information Oliver could use. Roy, how do you figure the employees learned that Shellenbach knew about the illegality?"

"They monitored Lodge One with their own Big Ear."

"There's a big hole in that unless Shellenbach monologued aloud or talked in his sleep. It's more logical to assume they overheard him confide to Noornan—or the reverse, Noornan to him."

Raber began to tap the desk with a forefinger.

"Shellenbach was a newcomer to Twin Springs. Noornan had been there before and knew the setup under the Barringtons. Let's assume Noornan is nosy. She's the athletic type, alone in Lodge Twelve. It's night, she's bored and restless. She goes outside and wanders down to the parking lot behind her lodge. Or she goes there on purpose. It's warm and quiet. She hears voices from a screened porch at the north end of the farmhouse. What's the distance interval, a hundred feet? She overhears Palan and Goodone discussing this illegal business. They are city men. They have no idea how clearly ordinary conversation carries on a quiet night in the country. Noornan—"

Raber banged a fist on the desk.

"Damn, it's been right before my stupid eyes!"

He pulled open a desk drawer, found a long ruler, and laid it atop the desk blotter.

"Below Lodge Twelve a lane runs to the landing field used by the helicopter. The ruler is that lane."

He set Big Ear parallel to the ruler.

"Big Ear is a long unused stable parallel to the lane with the farmhouse behind it. This morning I noticed that the Dutch doors on the stable facing the lane sagged on their hinges and one set was fully open. Now, back to Noornan. She sneaks across the lane, enters the stable by that opened door, and inches to the rear of the stall. At the back are sliding windows. We assume one is ajar. Where is she now? Twenty feet from the two key men on that screened porch."

Raber leaned forward tensely.

"She's in a perfect spot to eavesdrop and hear any incriminating talk. Maybe she returns a second night, even a third. Anyway, she learns the secret we're after. But she decides the matter is too big for her to handle. Shellenbach arrived at Lodge One on Monday, September third. Make no mistake about this. Almost immediately she made a strong play for him. Sex followed that first night at Lodge One and afterward they became inseparable. Now, we easily unmasked Shellenbach as a private detective. Using sex, she picked his brains and tipped him to the illegality. They became allies. If that gang had a listening device and tuned in on Lodge One or Twelve, they learned that Noornan and Shellenbach had discovered their real business in coming to Twin Springs."

Raber leaned back in the chief's swivel chair.

"That's a lot of if's," Boyce commented. "It may explain why Shellenbach visited us on September sixth and tried to pump us for information about the employees. Those two found themselves in over their depth."

Raber shrugged. "You two care to kick that theory around?"

For quite some time Sprague had sat silent. Now he hunched forward and said, "I don't like it."

"The theory is illogical?" Boyce demanded.

"No, it's too damned logical. The employees learned that Noornan and Shellenbach knew what went on at Twin Springs wasn't just running a fancy trout club. To shut

Shellenbach up they murder him and arrange a drowning to look like an accident. Now, do they let Noornan run free? Because she's an old guest? Because she's a female? Because she's stacked? Because she'll keep her mouth shut?"

Sprague answered his own questions.

"Like hell they let her run free! That's why she's gone from the club. When and if we locate her, we find her dead, murdered and rigged to look like another accident."

Raber dug into it.

"If Shellenbach worked alone, the employees couldn't possibly have found out he knew about their illegality. Noornan had to be involved. It makes no difference, now, which one first uncovered the illegality. Or who made the decision for Shellenbach to visit us."

Raber studied Sprague.

"You're a good man to have on our side because you put everything in sharp focus. Frankly, I've been clinging to hope. When we find Noornan.... Wait till the chief arrives home on Monday and we dump two unsolved murders in his lap!"

Raber rose abruptly.

"Dick, tag these items and place them in the safe. Roy, can you be here tomorrow morning at ten o'clock?"

"Sure, what's up ahead?"

"We'll give Big Ear a more thorough testing. If we decide to use it at Twin Springs, we'll know its capabilities even though what we hear won't be worth a legal damn. Tomorrow maybe the cotenant will be back at London Terrace. Meanwhile I'll dig deeper into Noornan."

"How will you do that?" Sprague asked.

"By talking to the Barringtons," Raber said, and he and Boyce went outside into the late-afternoon warmth.

"Do you think their New York City lawyer, Oppenheim, is running the show?" Boyce wondered.

"No, he's out of touch." Raber opened the door of his unmarked car. "Gene Palan is the boss."

"What are you withholding, Fred?"

"Palan controls the purse strings at Twin Springs. How did I know about those two padlocks on that new room in the basement? Jack Pelter told me. He read their water meter on September first. That hatch door was locked and Jack knew it hadn't been locked before. Joe Arragon picked Jack up and stood him against a town truck. Arragon told Jack not to enter the basement. To protect himself Jack grabbed a wrench from the truck, the type used to turn a hydrant off or on. Palan arrived and sent Arragon on his way. That's the boss, making a decision. Jack threatened to turn off their waterline with that wrench, which was impossible to do. So Palan unlocked the hatch door from the inside. Jack read the meter and told me about the two padlocks on that new room. He also gave me the idea for the Hicksville ploy this morning."

"How?"

"Jack was amused because Palan thought that wrench could turn off the water main. He said it was easy for hicks like us to fool smarties from the city."

Raber slid behind the wheel and closed the car door.

"That's why Hicksville worked for us."

He started the engine.

"Fred, weren't you supposed to take Elise and the children on a picnic today?"

Raber nodded and backed the car into Mercer Street.

"Roy, resign from the force while you're still young. All I've had to eat since an early breakfast has been coffee."

Raber headed for home.

10

On sunday afternoon, September 9, Fred Raber turned off Haycock Road, eased past a white farmhouse, and parked near a red barn where a man in his sixties loafed on a chaise lounge under a sugar maple. Raber walked up to him.

"Captain, it's good to see you again," John Barrington offered cordially. "I won't get up, I'm on vacation."

"You remain comfortable," Raber said as they shook hands.

"Buy you a drink?"

"No, thanks."

"Hah, that means you're on duty."

Barrington waved to a chair and Raber sat down.

"This is business, right?"

"No, it's largely pleasure. Is Mrs. Barrington around?"

"She's off visiting relatives. Yesterday morning early I heard all the sirens up the road. That's grim, a drowning at the club. You know what?" Barrington waggled a forefinger. "They should stop the swimming there. The spring water's deep and cold. It's that drowning brought you here, right?"

"No, it's a small matter, really. When you sold the club to Empire, did you include your jeep?"

"Right."

"We received a complaint. The new owners drive the jeep off the premises, but failed to obtain new plates."

"That's hogwash and sounds like Joel Futterman up the road. Hell, he's always wrong. I removed the plates from the jeep." Barrington gestured toward the barn. "I nailed 'em to a wall. Care to check?"

"Your word is good enough for me."

"Last week I saw the jeep in town and it has new plates."

"Thanks for the information and that ends the business."

Raber edged toward the reason for his visit. "Are you enjoying a vacation?"

"Sure in hell am, relaxing and fishing." Barrington indicated the brook beyond the barn. "That's a fine head of water from the pond. Captain, I built four rock dams in April and stocked the pools with big goldens, old-fashioneds, and rainbows."

"You have occasion to visit the club?"

"Me?" Barrington snorted. "When I drive past the club, I always look east at our twenty acres." He lowered his voice. "In strict confidence, the new owners are headed for trouble."

"Really?"

Raber knew the man liked the sound of his own voice and the strategy was to give him plenty of line.

"Yep, they're headed for trouble. Martha and I ran the whole shebang with help from the Luke Colters. They lived upstairs in the barn. They were good workers and knew the ropes. Empire acted like fools to let them go. We raised new stock, mended the road, painted, repaired, and Martha ran the office. Luke's wife cleaned the lodges and even washed the dirty linen. Today, captain? There's five of them, strong and lazy. They even send out the linen to Ajax in Suffern."

Barrington turned reflective.

"In this business you learn to pare down the overhead. Save the pennies, I always say, and the dollars mount in the bank. So they're in a peck of trouble and not from high overhead, either."

Raber waited, the patient fisherman.

"There are six big bedrooms upstairs in the farmhouse," Barrington continued. "During the rush seasons, I rented those rooms to overflow guests. Them? They bunk three employees in six rooms. I rented that nice apartment in the barn in rush seasons and the Colters slept in our living room. Hell, now their chef sleeps there alone."

Raber prodded: "Headed for financial trouble, are they?"

"Toward less net profit, captain. They're booked solid, even have some foreign fishermen. They ferry 'em to and from Philly in that rented helicopter and the foreigners only stay two or three days."

"The pilot just operates the helicopter?"

"Mostly, and he's a sour, lazy hulk built like a tank. Captain, the real business of Empire is export and import and Paul Goodone runs that. Their headquarters is in Jersey City and they expedite air freight with branch offices overseas. It must be profitable, too." Barrington smiled. "They introduced a new wrinkle. I shouldn't tell this, you're police. I thought my rich guests only wanted to relax and hook into some big trout. Now a guest can hook into something fancier than a six-pound rainbow, say a sexy young call girl, at a hundred bucks per night. Maybe for two nights or a week, if a guest is up to it. Hell, I never thought of that wrinkle, but Martha wouldn't have allowed it."

"For a man who looks east whenever he drives past the club," Raber suggested, "you seem to know the club's entire operation."

"I made damned sure of that," Barrington said and winked. "Per the contract terms, I mailed out announcements of the new ownership to all my clients. You know, the same fine service at the best private trout-fishing club in the East. You don't know that Oppenheim, a city lawyer who handled the deal for Empire. Twice he was a guest and he sure fancies himself. He's a pompous ass, him and his bow tie! He had all the answers for a Fair Hills hick."

Barrington chuckled.

"If they default on the mortgage payments, we get the club right back, that's how dumb we are! Captain, I've known some of those guests since the club opened. I wrote on some announcements we lived just down the road and drop in for a snort. And they do, fishermen are great drinkers. They talk your head off, like last Sunday when a woman came by, Evelyn Noornan, from New York City. She's a buyer for Lord & Taylor. She jabbered for two hours, even asked about the local police and I said they were good. Yep, I know where the mice feed at the club."

"Noornan is an unusual surname," Raber murmured,

tightening the line. "Are you putting me on, a New York City woman who fishes?"

"She's better than some of the males, learned as a teenager in Michigan. An uncle taught her and she never lost the urge."

"Mr. Barrington, you make her sound interesting."

"That's a mild adjective, captain. She's tall and weighs a hundred thirty pounds. She's strong, quick, and graceful. She's in the early thirties and unmarried. She's a brunette and tanned, I bet every damn square inch! She always wore a bikini, even in cool weather. I let her swim in that cold water because she's a regular seal."

Barrington smacked his lips.

"She drove up in a new Corvette, but she's not a good driver. *Wham!* She wore a bikini and I watched that lush figure trying to fight its way out from two skimpy pieces of cloth! She always had a lodge to herself, usually Twelve, and the males sniffed around, you bet. I think some of them made out, too, but not at a hundred bucks per night. She is a generous woman, but don't get the wrong idea, captain. She is high-class, even if Martha doesn't cotton to her."

"What is Martha's reason?" Raber asked casually.

"I think Martha is just scratching, like an envious cat. She says Evelyn is the nosiest female she ever met, asking intimate questions, poking around the club, here and there." Barrington laughed. "Hell, Evelyn can ask me how often I wee just so long as she's wearing one of those bikinis!"

Raber rose.

"Mr. Barrington, thanks for the information about the jeep. You saved me a visit to the club and a red face. I enjoyed the conversation. Tell Mrs. Barrington how sorry I was to miss her."

"Right. You like to fish?"

"I know a trout's head from its tail."

"Hah, like the new club's owners! If you change your mind, try my new pools for free."

"Thank you."

Raber started off, then turned back.

"I enjoyed the visit so much I forgot to mention some

news. Remember how we patrolled the club four or five times a week?"

"That was nice of you, too. Local fishermen knew about those unscheduled patrols and it stopped all the poaching."

"In April the new owners ordered us to stop."

"That's stupid." Barrington rubbed his face. "They gave a reason?"

"Mr. Palan said that any police patrol would disturb the bucolic atmosphere of the club." Raber smiled easily. "Besides the husky employees, do they have any other security, say a police dog?"

"No dogs, that's for sure. It's no problem to poach if locals don't sneak in from Haycock Road."

"What blocks the front?"

"Well, at night the main entrance is trapped with a photoelectric eye. If anybody goes through, in a car or on foot, a bell rings in the office. They better avoid that chain-link fence for a hundred fifty yards north and south of the entrance, too. After dark it carries a light electric charge. Say a deer brushes against that fence and a buzzer sounds in the office. That's a waste of money, captain."

"Probably. The measures are a form of security?"

"Or stupidity. Want to know how I found out?"

Raber nodded.

"The new owners use my electrical contractor, Sam Breadon, from Suffern. I met Sam in May and he told me about the two new jobs. Sam said they toss their money around and weren't like me. Sam thinks they are nuts and so do I."

This time Raber boarded the unmarked car and left.

At Twin Springs, how nosy had Evelyn Noornan been?

More important, since she was an amateur, had she stumbled somewhere and been murdered?

11

On Monday morning, September 10, standing inside the door of a Georgian house, Mrs. Henry McCartney overheard a shortwave call emanating from an unmarked police car parked at the front curb. She hurried through the extensive house to a sunroom at the rear where Fred Raber watched Roy Boyce start to lift another fingerprint from the sash of a broken window.

"Captain," she explained, "someone is trying to raise you on shortwave and it sounds important."

Raber said, "Thanks," and strode from the house. At the car he said into the mike: "Raber. Yes?"

Officer Nosse answered: "You wanted to be reminded of coffee break. How soon, please?"

"I'll lunch instead. Seven minutes. Out."

Back in the sunroom, Mrs. McCartney asked, "Was it important?"

"It seems I missed my coffee break."

"But I'd have brewed coffee!"

Boyce said, "Don't bother," and studied a print. "Clear, like the other two. Captain, if these prints are on file anywhere, we're home free on this rip job. Amateurs, probably." He smiled reassuringly at Mrs. McCartney. "A thousand-to-one odds against another job here. Captain, I'll complete the inventory of stolen articles. And lunch at HQ, say in twenty minutes?"

Raber nodded, then told Mrs. McCartney, "Don't worry, please."

In the car, he drove fast, without siren or blinkers. "Coffee break" translated into "Urgent, you are needed at HQ." This was Zone 1, northeast sector, the McCartney rip the third in this outlying area within two months. All isolated houses. All in midmorning. All with the occupants temporarily away.

Was the rip job a drug addict after a quick buck? That was a distinct possibility. As soon as the probationary offices were able to man the desk alone, several officers would be freed to enter vulnerable areas and organize the residents into groups who would report all strange cars to headquarters.

He entered Mercer Street from the east, parked by the Municipal Building, and noted a strange car with New York State plates. Upstairs, Sande Nosse was alone at the desk.

"Lieutenant Sprague took an early lunch," she explained. "A stranger, Miss Adele Myrick is here. She may be twenty-five years old and weighs less than a hundred pounds. She's a blonde with blue eyes and very attractive with a helpless attitude. She hinted at a need for police assistance, us or the State Police. I served coffee and explained Chief Hocking was busy in court. I suggested pulling you in and she agreed to wait. She's a clam, captain."

"Where is she?"

"In the powder room. She is obviously upset and had been crying earlier. Her problem seemed urgent. I suggested she fix her face and you'd be here within minutes. She puzzled me."

"I'll talk to her in the chief's office," Raber decided. "After the introduction, close the door as you leave."

"Of course."

In the chief's office, he switched on a subdued overhead light and a desk lamp. Off one desk corner, he arranged a chair and placed the chief's swivel chair opposite it. Voices sounded outside.

"Miss Myrick," Nosse enthused, "you are stunning!"

"Thank you," a tiny voice answered. "And thanks for your attention and the delicious coffee."

Nosse ushered her in, murmured, "Miss Myrick, our Captain Raber," and left, closing the door.

She was beautiful, probably photogenic, Raber decided, petite, blond hair perfectly in place. The blue eyes were alert and watchful. A neat figure graced a high-collared white shirtwaist and she wore an exquisitely tailored lightweight knit suit in gray with pinpoints of bright color.

"My pleasure," Raber said politely.

"How do you do, captain."

"If you'll be seated, please?"

It was an excellent performance.

First she shifted a white strap purse to her left shoulder. She sat in a fluid, practiced movement, buttocks forward on the chair, body erect up through the shoulders, nyloned knees pressed together, right leg slanting left, the other leg tucked behind it, and red shoes, the left one behind the right.

She studied Raber, then said in a tiny voice, "I find myself pleasantly surprised."

"In what way?"

"I had expected a much older, larger man. In uniform. With a stiff solemn face. And wearing a gold badge."

"We're quite casual around here, Miss Myrick."

Raber sat, no barrier between them. Leaning back, he crossed one leg at the knee, rested elbows on the chair arms, and joined his fingertips loosely at chest height. He began to talk, easily and quietly, a sales pitch designed to unravel her story because pride forced him in that direction.

"Conditions have changed around police stations, Miss Myrick. For the better, we hope."

He smiled, as she was still too tense in her facial expression and her fingers fiddled with her purse.

"We like the pastel wall colors and good prints, like that Corot copy." His hands opened expansively. "We like an informal atmosphere with no disturbing elements because relaxation is the key to the solution of any personal problem. With visitors, we offer courteous and prompt service, whether we confer with local taxpayers or strangers. Also, we hope our service is efficient."

Again he smiled, this time across his joined fingertips.

"Our breed is changing, perhaps not as rapidly as it should, but higher education is becoming a prerequisite for an officer of the law. I went to Rutgers University and five of our officers are enrolled at a local community college. We also added three women to the force. The other two are as capable as Officer Nosse. Shall I sum up what she told me?"

"Please."

"We know your name. You have a problem that may

require our attention or that of the State Police. You will make that decision, correct?"

She nodded.

"It is not necessary to offer further information, not even your address. To aid you in reaching a decision I have considerable information on tap. Our department consists of twenty-three women and men headed by Chief Hocking. Every hour, day and night, we are responsible for the protection of seventeen thousand residents in our hundred square miles, which is rather woolly in spots. About eight hundred residents commute to New York City, but we are essentially an unsophisticated town. In handling a problem, we have two advantages over other police authorities. We know every square mile of our territory. We know every resident and strangers as such. During the course of our work, these are plus factors. As an illustration of our capability, in answer to Officer Nosse's summons, I left another case and arrived here within seven minutes. Parked outside is a 1971 Chrysler, New Yorker model, dark blue, New York State license number 278-3N91, rented from a national agency that does not need to work harder because it is already number one. You arrived in that car?"

She nodded.

"Let me be a bit presumptuous. I suggest you live in New York City. You are highly sophisticated. You are tastefully dressed. My guess is that you are a professional model. It showed in your walk and in those neat quarter-turns. It showed in the way you sat—no, in the way you ensconced yourself in the chair. Hours of disciplined training sustain your erect carriage and I believe the correct term is steel holding the curves in place. You offer an outward softness that I find appealing, yet I suggest you have great inner strength to enable you to meet your present problem. Do you live in New York City?"

"Yes."

"Are you a professional model?"

"Yes."

"To help you solve your present problem, let us consider the New Jersey State Police, with whom I worked for three years before coming here. They are an organized, disciplined, efficient group with an excellent officer corps and investigative staff. Their advantage over us is that they have authority anywhere in the state. If you decide to seek their cooperation, Miss Myrick, I shall take you to the nearest barracks, introduce you to the captain, and leave."

Uncrossing his leg, Raber leaned forward.

"I suggest you avail yourself of all the information I have on tap, then make your decision. Consider the Telford County Investigative Staff. Our authority stops at the limits of Fair Hills, unless we are engaged in close pursuit. Which is not true of the county. They pass freely across the borders of fifty-six municipalities. They have a top investigative staff, headed by Major Orwell, a personal friend. If you select them to assist you, I shall drive you to Ardnor, the county seat, and entrust you to the major's competent care. Miss Myrick, I am not trying to complicate your decision, but do not overlook the Federal Bureau of Investigation. Many citizens have the quaint idea that their problems must be big and important before the FBI enters. This is the determining factor: Has a state line been crossed? If this is true in your case, we shall have an agent here within two hours to accommodate your needs. This morning, what time did you leave New York City?"

"Very early, seven o'clock."

"If you don't object, under what circumstances?"

"I—I did not sleep well—I was too distraught."

"And?"

"I—I left to meet a New York State trooper at the bridge."

"Ah, you mean Tappan Zee Bridge?"

She nodded.

"At the toll booths, *this* side of the Hudson River?"

"Yes, a very polite young man."

She was putty in his skilled hands, being interrogated, but not realizing it, and he said gently, "At seven o'clock this morning, you were able to rent the Chrysler from a Hertz Agency?"

"Oh, no!" The words tumbled out. "I returned last night. A week's vacation in Maine with my parents. At the airport I rented the Chrysler. This morning it was still in my possession."

"Why did you leave so early?"

"Mail had accumulated and I had gone over it last night. There were two memos to phone a certain number, the—the New York State Police. I did so immediately. There had been a car accident and—and—"

She verged on tears.

"This accident involved someone else's car?" Raber said soothingly.

She shook her head, striving for control.

"To your car?"

"Yes."

"And your car is?"

"A—a Corvette."

"You're doing fine, Miss Myrick. Who was operating your car?"

"My cotenant."

"Had the State Police already identified her?"

"No, only my ownership."

"Now, you met this polite young trooper at the bridge. Where did he escort you?"

"To Suffern."

"Where the accident had taken place?"

She inhaled raggedly and nodded.

"Do you know the time of the accident?"

"Two A.M."

"What day, please?"

"On—on Saturday."

"You are doing fine, Miss Myrick. The accident occurred at two A.M., on Saturday, September eighth. Do you know the location?"

"Route Seventeen and the D-Dewey Thruway."

"At Suffern did you meet someone else?"

"A-a man named Belding."

"He would be Captain Belding, a fine officer, in charge of their local barracks. If you feel up to it, just one more question. You were asked to identify your cotenant?"

"I—she—her face—"

With no warning, the steel that supported her curves buckled. She pitched forward. Raber caught her with his right hand. With his left hand he opened the door.

"Nosse!"

The officer hurried in.

"She's fainted," Raber snapped. "Pry her feet apart."

Nosse knelt on the rug.

"Now separate her knees about four inches."

Nosse did and Raber lowered the woman's head into the space between her opened knees. Holding her with one hand, he moved behind the chair, placed his hands on the nape of her neck, with a thumb flat on either side of the spinal cord, and massaged upward.

"That's to restore circulation. You take over."

Nosse switched positions with Raber.

"Don't you let her fall, officer."

"I won't."

Raber rummaged in the chief's desk and located a bottle of four-star brandy and a plastic jigger. He decanted an ounce, then returned the bottle for the next emergency.

"Did she tell you her troubles, captain?"

"It wasn't necessary."

Adele Myrick moaned. Holding her by the shoulders, Nosse elevated her into a sitting position. She opened her eyes and Nosse asked the traditional question: "Miss Myrick, are you all right?"

"I fainted!"

"That's all right."

"I feel so silly!"

"You faced a crisis bravely," Raber told her. "This is brandy, it will help."

She sipped from the jigger and swallowed.

"One more," Raber ordered.

She sipped again and exclaimed, "It warmed me clear down to my belly button!"

They all laughed.

"Officer," Raber directed, "I'll take a brief intermission. Will Mr. Boyce be in his office?"

"Yes."

"You stay with Miss Myrick. She's a professional model. Talk about that."

In the back area, Roy Boyce sat drinking coffee.

"Sande said the visitor is a beautiful blonde," Boyce grinned. "My boss always gets the cushy jobs."

"She's Adele Myrick and she's Evelyn Noornan's cotenant."

"What's my job?"

"Noornan is at Layton's Mortuary in Suffern. She had a fatal accident in Myrick's Corvette at two A.M., Saturday, at the junction of Route Seventeen and the Thruway."

Boyce rose promptly.

"Those callous bastards. It's another murder one."

"First you check, then you conclude," Raber warned. "The New York State troopers handled the accident. Mistaken identity was involved. Ownership of the Corvette was established, but not that of the corpse. Evidently the police held back a complete news release until they established the identity of the corpse and Miss Myrick did that early this morning."

"And?"

"Get up to Suffern. It's not our bailiwick, so you need a cover."

"I won't play a car insurance rep," Boyce decided. "Umm, what about this? I'm a Prudential agent. We hold a small life insurance policy on the deceased and need full particulars on the accident."

"Okay, but take your own car. Phone the Suffern police and locate where the tow truck took the Corvette. You understand cars. Find out if that Corvette was rigged to look like an accident. You dig, but I want you back within an hour."

"You know it's our job all the way, Fred."

"Why?"

"They murdered her at Twin Springs and it's another rig job."

"Prove it," Raber said, and left.

12

AS SHE left the chief's office, Officer Nosse closed the door and Raber asked: "Miss Myrick, what have you eaten today?"

"I've had a cup of coffee and that jigger of brandy."

"Across the street we have a small, excellent restaurant. Will you be my guest?"

"First I must explain fully the reason for my visit here."

Raber said, "We'll postpone the food," and sat in a swivel chair.

"It's very involved," she warned.

"There's no hurry."

"Until I identified Evelyn at the morgue, the police thought she was I. That's understandable because all they had for identification were the Corvette's plates and the owner's certificate in the glove compartment. They were kind and I signed a paper. I explained to Captain Belding that Evelyn had been vacationing at Twin Springs Trout Club in Fair Hills. I thought I should drive there and collect her things and he agreed."

"What is Evelyn's surname?"

"Oh, dear!" she exclaimed. "I omitted her surname, didn't I? It's Noornan."

"To me, Twin Springs suggests that she was fishing."

"That's right."

"Was she good at the sport?"

"She was an expert and equally avid."

"Was she a career woman like yourself?"

"Yes, she was a buyer of women's accessories at Lord & Taylor. Oh, she was seven years older than I. We rented an apartment jointly and lived together for two years." Her blue eyes were guileless. "We were lovers and that's why I was so upset, captain."

"I understand," Raber said quickly. "Did you know the route from Suffern to Twin Springs?"

"No, because we never drove the Thruway to reach the club from the city. That's why I'm so positive that—"

Raber lifted a hand.

"Miss Myrick, let's keep your explanation in sequence. Develop the facts, then draw the inferences afterward, okay?"

"That's more logical," she agreed. "That polite young trooper escorted me over the state line to Route Seventeen and it was a simple matter to reach your Broad Street and continue to the club along our usual route. I knew the Barringtons had sold the club in April, but I had not yet met the new owners. I met a very nice man, a Mr. Palan. He was shocked to learn the news of Evelyn's death. He explained that a ringing phone in the office had awakened him after twelve o'clock on Friday night. The caller was a man. Mr. Palan made the connection to Lodge Twelve so that's how I'm positive—oh, I'm sorry! Mr. Palan said he had heated a glass of milk and heard the Corvette start up nearby. He thought Evelyn might need some assistance and stepped outside. Evelyn told him she had been called unexpectedly to the city and would return in a day or so. He accompanied me to Lodge Twelve where she usually stayed. I was terribly distraught and packed her things. I would have overlooked her fishing gear, except for Mr. Palan. He loaded everything in the Chrysler's back seat. I thanked him, started off, and—"

"One point," Raber interrupted. "I'm interested in Miss Noonan's purse containing her driver's license and identification. Her purse wasn't found in the Corvette?"

"I omitted that detail, didn't I? Of all places, I found her purse in her bedroom. I followed our regular route toward the city; that is, south on Route Seventeen to the cloverleaf at Route Four, east to the George Washington Bridge, then downtown on the West Side Highway. That is the shortest, most convenient route which we always followed. Now, I was still on Route Seventeen. Suddenly, everything became clearer. You see, my sanity had returned. I parked on the shoulder and thought and thought. Afterward, I circled the cloverleaf and drove here."

She sat relaxed, now in full control of her emotions.

"Captain, here are my inferences. Because of our relationship, I knew no man would have phoned Evelyn after midnight. Besides, no man outside the club knew where she was on Friday night. She had me, you understand, and I had her. She rarely concerned herself with men. If a man had telephoned, I can't imagine any urgency that would have sent her rushing off alone after midnight. And leaving her purse behind? Heavens, the bridge toll on the Thruway, Captain Belding explained, is a dollar and the police didn't find a dime in the Corvette!"

She paused to adjust the hemline of her skirt.

"Yet, there was her purse left behind at Lodge Twelve. While I sat thinking, I opened her purse. It contained her driver's license, adequate identification such as four credit cards, considerable change, and eighty-four dollars in bills. Evelyn is meticulous and her purse is part of her. Do you understand, captain?"

"Yes—Mrs. Raber's purse is an extension of her hands."

"Precisely! And why would Evelyn drive north on Route Seventeen, a route we never took? If she had planned to enter the city, via the Thruway, that meant more unfamiliar driving to London Terrace. Somebody was unaware of our normal route to Twin Springs and that somebody was unfamiliar with something even more important!"

She leaned forward from the hips.

"Captain Belding explained the Corvette hurdled a low barrier on Route Seventeen, slammed into a pillar that supported the overhead Thruway, and the speedometer jammed at seventy. I know Evelyn never drove that fast! In fact, she didn't like to drive my Corvette. While she fished at Twin Springs, I vacationed with my parents in Maine. I didn't want to leave the new Corvette in a garage and had to force Evelyn to take it with her. Captain, I'll sum up the inferences. I cannot imagine Evelyn, minus purse and driver's license and money, late at night, driving an unfamiliar route, answering an unexplained urgency, telephoned by a man who could not possibly have known where she was, traveling at such a terrific speed, and crashing to her death."

"Nicely summarized," Raber approved. "What is your conclusion?"

"This was not an accidental death. For some unknown reasons, somebody murdered Evelyn."

"So you came to us?"

Easily she retreated into her little girl role.

"That is the reason," she said in a tiny voice. "Please, will you help me?"

"We'll launch an immediate investigation," he promised. "However, you offered no evidence that will stand up in court. There are many unexplained points in your story, even large holes, plus the absence of a convincing motive."

He rose and smiled.

"Miss Myrick, let's take time out. What you need is some food added to the brandy and coffee in your stomach."

"But I'm not the least bit hungry!"

"Then join me. I haven't eaten since an early breakfast."

They entered headquarters where Raber told Officer Nosse, "We're adjourning to the restaurant. Have Mr. Boyce join us, please."

"Yes, sir."

They sat at a rear table in the restaurant and dined leisurely on homemade soup, tuna sandwiches, and coffee.

"What about an excellent dessert?" Raber suggested.

"No, I count calories and watch my figure."

"So that other people will watch it?"

"I like your deft touch!"

She chose chocolate cake, as he did, and ate her entire portion, then lit a cigarette, inhaled, and let smoke sit in her lungs.

"You intrigue me," Raber offered.

"Because I flaunt medical advice on smoking?"

"No, the ease with which you project a helpless attitude when you are quite the opposite. Why do you drive a powerful Corvette?"

"It's physical ambivalence," she said cryptically, and stretched her right hand across the table. "Shake, partner."

He discovered that her fingers were surprisingly strong, her palm calloused, and more strength generated from her wrist.

"Femininity is a prerequisite in my modeling," she noted. "On the job, my physical strength is easily masked. Why do I drive a Corvette? It's a release. Evelyn said I should drive a Grand Prix. I get a lift from all that horsepower at my fingertips. You practically sit on the road, something that scared the hell out of Evelyn. Eighty or ninety miles an hour? I just soar and soar."

Roy Boyce found them still holding hands.

Raber made the introductions, merely saying, "Mr. Boyce," and to him she became the little girl. A waitress served coffee all around.

"Any progress?" Raber asked, and Boyce nodded.

"Miss Myrick," Raber continued, "you have certain responsibilities. Who's the nearest of kin to be notified?"

"Evelyn's parents are dead," she explained. "An uncle in Michigan raised her. I suspect he treated her like a nephew and taught her sports, including trout fishing."

"Would you consider not notifying this uncle for forty-eight hours?"

"Yes, if you have an adequate reason."

Raber sipped coffee, then set the cup down.

"Roy Boyce is a detective. While you were talking to Officer Nosse, I dispatched him to Suffern to check your Corvette." Raber shrugged. "We are involved with another police matter at the trout club that occurred on Saturday morning, September eighth. We have been trying for two days to reach Miss Noornan at the London Terrace address. So, we find ourselves in a bind and this other matter is sub rosa. We had thought that Miss Noornan might give us some relevant information. Will you trust us for forty-eight hours?"

"All along—good heavens!" she exclaimed. "I didn't tell you Evelyn's full name until after you had sent your detective to Suffern!"

"That's correct."

"When I arrived here, you already knew who I was?"

"No."
"But you did know Evelyn was dead!"
"No."
"I thought—we were two strangers—I withheld information—"
Helplessly, she turned to Boyce, "Is your captain psychic?"
"No, he's good with numbers. Once he told me most logic is based on arithmetic." Boyce displayed his cherubic smile. "When he adds two and two, the captain's answer is often five."
"When he talked to me earlier," she confided to Boyce, "he practically hypnotized me!"
"Please don't overdo the compliments. I have to live with him."
She studied Raber. "And I thought I was being so clever!"
Raber waited.
"My inferences were correct?"
"They are plausible, Miss Myrick, but that is not proof."
"Do you believe Evelyn was murdered?"
"Inferences too often lead to a hasty conclusion."
"Why would anyone want to murder Evelyn?"
"I suggest we listen to Detective Boyce's progress report. Let's have it, but not too grim."
"It's two A.M. on Saturday, September eighth," Boyce began. "There would be very little traffic on Route Seventeen, four lanes with a divider. That gave them an opportunity to maneuver on a straight stretch paralleling the Ford assembly plant, which was closed. Also, there are no homes in this area. Short of the plant, on my trip north, I checked the concrete surface. That is, the right-hand lane. I spotted two fresh wide treadmarks, as if a car had been gunned. I measured the width of those marks and later checked them against the Corvette's tires. They were roughly identical. Now, at high speed, the Corvette would run relatively true, even with no driver, because of power steering. At the inception of the first road curve, the Corvette hurdled a low barrier and crashed into a pillar of the overhead Thruway. Also, there were no treadmarks on the concrete that would occur if the power brakes had been applied.

Since Miss Noornan was found alone in the Corvette, I believe she was unconscious and unaware of the danger. The impact stalled the engine and no fire resulted. Later, I learned the speedometer needle was jammed at seventy miles an hour. Clear, Miss Myrick?"

She nodded.

"I located the Suffern garage where the Corvette had been towed. I wore civilian clothes and this was out of our jurisdiction. I posed as a life insurance agent. We had a policy on Miss Noornan and I needed more particulars on the accident. I received answers to questions; for example, the victim had not been using a seat belt. I inspected the Corvette alone. The front end was demolished and the battered hood fully sprung. The engine had been shoved backward three or four inches. The extension of the accelerator bar had been wired down with fine wire that would escape a cursory examination. I'd say the throttle was almost fully open. This would seem to be the MO. At Lodge Twelve, they quietly render Miss Noornan unconscious, place her on the Corvette's front seat, and may have covered her with a blanket. One man drives the Corvette onto the shoulder of Route Seventeen adjacent to those first treadmarks on the concrete. Change that to yards before the first treadmarks. A second car parks behind the Corvette, probably their Buick sedan because their jeep would be inappropriate for the job. The driver of the Corvette cuts the engine, lifts the hood, and wires the accelerator bar in place. For that job, I'd pick their helicopter pilot. Oh—anybody in a passing car would think they had engine trouble and keep going. The wiring job might take two minutes. Now, all windows are closed on the Corvette except the one by the driver's seat, and the air-conditioning unit is set on cool. The driver places Miss Noornan behind the wheel or near it. They're ready. The driver reaches inside and starts the engine. It must have gone off with a roar. He steers the Corvette and the Buick pushes it onto the road. He lines the Corvette for a straight course. Since the Buick's front bumper is higher than that of the Corvette, it should have left marks on the paint of the new Corvette. When I checked the outside of the Corvette later, there were the telltale marks from the car that had pushed. As the Corvette gains speed, the driver runs alongside. He aims the wheels straight. Now comes the tricky part, but it can be done. It's teamwork. He reaches inside and slips the Corvette into high gear. It takes off like a rocket. They get the hell out of there fast, probably cutting into the south lanes of Route Seventeen by a break in the divider fence used by police cars. Well?"

In the silence, Adele Myrick spoke first.

"Detective Boyce, you did a commendable job. I told Captain Raber earlier that under no circumstances would Evelyn ever have operated my car at such a high rate of speed because she was a poor driver. As for the Corvette? I have gunned it, almost full-throttle, from a stationary start with never a stall-out. And those two men had an added advantage as the pushing car acted as a booster."

She turned to Raber. "Do you know the identity of those two men?"

"No."

"Are they employees at Twin Springs?"

"I believe so."

"How many employees are there?"

"Five."

"And that nice Mr. Palan lied to me about Evelyn receiving a phone call after midnight on Friday night that sent her off?"

"I believe he lied."

"So?"

"We need time and luck," Raber said slowly.

"I thank you both for your cooperation."

She pushed back from the table and rose, as did they. She settled the strap of her purse over her left shoulder.

"Captain, I won't call Jeremiah French, Evelyn's uncle, for forty-eight hours. If necessary, you may have more time. May I trade my cooperation for the answers to several questions?"

"Certainly," Raber agreed.

"This other matter at Twin Springs is also a murder?"

"We think so."

"Did those men rig it to look like a murder?"

She has a keen mind, Raber thought, and said aloud, "Probably."

"You said earlier you lacked a motive for Evelyn's murder and said later she might have been able to give you important information about this other matter. You did not know Evelyn, and she had a characteristic that I did not like. She pried constantly into the personal lives of other people, particularly men. I mean residents at London Terrace. She tailed them. She busied herself unraveling what they did, where they went, their interests, and so on. She was clever at this and to my knowledge was never suspected or caught. Evelyn always explained her actions by saying she was bored and besides, this game enabled her to outwit men! At Twin Springs she would have had time on her hands and may have pried into the lives of the employees. Judging from the events on Route Seventeen, these men sound like professionals, as does Mr. Palan with his easy lies. Evelyn was an amateur. If she pried at Twin Springs and learned something these men did not want an outsider to know, I think you may have the motive for her murder."

She started across the restaurant, now beginning to fill with customers, and she placed each red shoe, one ahead of the other, in an imaginary, straight line.

Boyce muttered, "She's quite a woman," and Raber nodded absently.

He left a tip, paid the tab at the cashier's desk, and crossed Mercer Street where he joined Boyce at the Chrysler. Adele Myrick sat behind the wheel, the car window open and the engine idling.

"Nice meeting you two," she said, reverting to her tiny voice. "If I were an employee at that trout club, I wouldn't want you on my trail."

She backed into Mercer Street and cut the wheels.

"I'm not too familiar with this car," she noted.

"We accept no alibis," Boyce said.

Smiling, she suddenly gunned the engine in high gear. With the rear tires shrilling a protest, the Chrysler shot forward. A half block distant, car brakes slammed on. She angled the Chrysler left and catapulted out of sight.

"And I thought she was a helpless doll," Boyce said cheerfully. "I suggested those employees rendered Noornan unconscious at Lodge Twelve. Not a chance, that ploy on Route Seventeen posed too many risks. They murdered her at the club and it's our job all the way."

"I agree, Roy. We'll drop this in the chief's lap and he'll confer with Captain Belding on the New York State angles. Is there any chance the employee who did the wiring job wore gloves?"

"No, because that wire is very fine and he had to work fast. Also, he probably thought they'd get away with it. There was a grease film on the extension of that accelerator bar. Belding's technicians may be able to pick up a fingerprint there and other places on the Corvette."

They hurried inside the building.

13

"FRED," BOYCE whispered, "it's almost ten o'clock. . . . Well?"

"Dull," Raber said, returning the whisper. "Arragon asked the chef if he'd taken his medicine and the chef said not yet. Everything else has been small talk."

They were lurking opposite the farmhouse at Twin Springs Trout Club, Monday night, September 10. They were on the property of the Barringtons, west of Haycock Road, hidden within a thick stand of bushes, and wore baseball caps and dark clothes. Boyce was monitoring Big Ear beamed at the target.

"Locate them," Raber hissed.

"Palan, downstairs quarters, drapes drawn. Arragon upstairs. Chef in kitchen. Krauthof and Goodone, off in the copter."

"Poor night," Raber decided and picked up a bamboo fishing rod. "Give me twenty minutes."

"An act of trespass?"

"I want to check out one item."

Raber edged from the bushy screen, retreated to the nearby brook, and followed a discernible path toward the Barringtons' farmhouse. Water gurgled over rock dams. Crickets chirruped a steady farewell to summer. Short of the lighted farmhouse, he swung west and slipped through the woods to Haycock Road. He was opposite the chain-link fence, electrically charged at night, where it terminated at a low post-and-rail fence inset with a white gate wide enough to let a car through. A row of sugar maples planted inside the charged fence stretched past the farmhouse where a shaded light glowed on a screened porch. Crossing the road swiftly, he vaulted the low gate and landed softly. To his left stretched another railed fence and he used this to screen his advance to a small landing field used by the helicopter. He turned left onto a lane that paralleled more fencing clear to its juncture with the north end of the unused horse stable.

In the quiet night, lit by high-riding stars and a waning moon, the stench of oil and gasoline from the landing field was strong. Within woods on the terminus of a slope, lights glowed in Lodge Twelve, newcomers here for the fall fishing. Insects shrilled, ceasing as he advanced and resuming after his passage. A little screech owl launched into its song and he thought that rather pleasant. Bending low, he reached the stable and paused by the first Dutch door.

There had been a change since Saturday.

All six doors now stood closed. He examined the first door, both units flush with the jamb. Starlight glinted off the heads of freshly set nails. He advanced cautiously. Every door was nailed shut.

Hmmm, belated insurance? he thought.

Reasonable, now, to assume that the employees had figured Evelyn Noornan had listened from the formerly opened stable and, a mere twenty feet from the screened porch had overheard conversation not intended for her ears?

He listened for a moment. He heard the splashing of the fountains that fed fresh water into the trout-breeding pools around the corner of the barn, eased around that corner for a look and—with no warning bumped into the bulk of Joe Arragon.

They were both startled, but Raber reacted more quickly. With both hands he brought up the fishing rod and slammed it against Arragon's chin. There was the sharp crack of breaking bamboo. The man lifted his hands belatedly and Raber dropped the rod. Turning, he raced along the stable.

"Diego!" Arragon called, his soft voice a roar. "Gino, Gino!"

From inside the farmhouse answering shouts sounded.

"Gino, bring a gun!" Arragon yelled.

At the end of the stable Raber chose boldness. Placing one hand on the fence's top rail, he vaulted cleanly and sprinted across a lawn that abutted the screened porch.

"What's up, Joe?" Palan shouted.

"Guy with a fishing rod. I almost nabbed him!"

"Where'd he go?"

"Toward the road!"

"After him in the jeep."

At the electrically charged fence, four feet high, Raber did not hesitate. With both hands, he grabbed the top and swung over. His sneakers made no sound as he darted across the macadam and gained the protection of the woods. It was reasonable for them to think that he had a car parked farther north. So he headed toward Boyce and heard the buzz of an alarm inside the farmhouse and then the roar of the jeep starting up somewhere near the barn.

He joined Boyce and hissed, "I blew it."

"So Big Ear told me. Did they make you?"

"No, I broke the rod on Arragon's jaw."

"Lie down, Fred," Boyce warned calmly.

With its headlights on, the jeep roared around the farmhouse, skidded through the entrance, and headed north.

"Let's move it," Raber whispered.

"The chef and Arragon are in the jeep—take it easy," Boyce said, and continued to monitor Big Ear.

Inside the office a bell rang, set off by the passage of the jeep through the entrance. Then, both buzzer and bell stopped. The seconds stole past.

"Where's Palan?" Raber urged.

Boyce did not answer. Then he clicked off the switch on Big Ear, removed the earphone from his head, and rose.

"Palan called the cops," he said, and chuckled. "Now we better get the hell out of here."

They hurried quietly through the woods, reached the outlet brook where they stopped by the bridge.

"It seems clear," Boyce decided, staring toward the farmhouse.

Then, off to the south, a siren sounded faintly.

"In Fair Hills," Boyce said, "the cops move fast."

They ran a hundred yards along Haycock Road, entered

110

a narrow wooded lane, and reached Raber's car, which was faced outward. The siren grew louder.

As they boarded the car with Raber behind the wheel, Raber decided, "It's Kelly coming in. He must have been in the northwest zone. I was stupid, they may stumble into our hideout."

"I doubt that. Anyway, Big Ear is good and tomorrow night we can hide deeper inside the woods."

"I learned what I wanted to know. They nailed those Dutch doors shut on the stable."

Its turret light revolving redly, siren at the crescendo, and headlights boring into the night, a squad car roared past.

Boyce laughed. "Mr. Palan, I call that prompt service."

Raber drove into Haycock Road and turned toward town.

"Stupid, stupid," he muttered.

At Harristown Road he turned right. Up ahead a second police car approached with the turret light turning.

"Probably the chief," Boyce said. "You flagging him down?"

"We'd better fill him in."

Raber switched on the red blinkers and stopped on the shoulder. The advancing car slowed and braked to a stop. Chief Hocking leaned from the open window of a squad car to demand, "You boys cause this alert?"

"There's no sweat," Boyce called across to him. "It was just an unknown poacher trying to fish in the breeding pools."

"Okay, I'll cover."

Hocking drove off.

At seven thirty on Tuesday night, September 11, in the chief's office, Laird Hocking studied Fred Raber and Roy Boyce, who were dressed in dark clothes preparatory for another surveillance at Twin Springs. The chief was in his late fifties, a big, wide-shouldered man with a solid face and graying hair.

"Last night you did no real harm," he said, seemingly enjoying Raber's discomfiture. "I told Mr. Palan that trespasser was only a stupid bungler." Hocking pointed to a broken bamboo fishing rod atop his desk. "Freddy, where'd you locate that?"

"It was with several others in the back area."

"I thought so. We confiscated those rods from poachers." Hocking leaned back in his swivel chair.

"Mr. Palan was pleasant, educated, and polite. I chatted about trout fishing and his knowledge on that subject could be stacked on the head of a pin. I explained the difference between sportsmen, like his guests, and a meat fisherman like the idiot Joe Arragon routed. He listened, but I doubt he was interested. I wanted to test him and explained that a sportsman uses a light rod, expensive tackle, and flies with small hooks to give the club's big trout a fighting chance. That's the art of the sport, unappreciated by Mr. Palan. A meat fisherman? He's after food for the table. He'll fish in breeding pools—with a net." Hocking chuckled. "Or a hammer. Both of you: Tonight stay the hell on Barrington's side of Haycock Road. Anything you learn using Big Ear as evidence isn't worth one dead trout."

Hocking picked up a sheaf of notes, shuffled through them, pausing here and there, then dropped them on the desk.

"I spent today in the company of a fine police officer, Jim Belding, captain, New York State Police. I explained we were already involved in a tough first-degree murder case at Twin Springs, said murder rigged to look like an accidental drowning. Jim understands we have to sit on that one—for a while. He already knew Evelyn Noornan was a guest at Twin Springs prior to the auto accident and I dropped the hint that she had been very close to the murdered man, also a guest. So, we took a closer look at that wrecked Corvette."

Hocking eyed Boyce.

"What I did *not* tell Jim was about the fine preliminary investigation you had already done. With no help from me Jim spotted the thin wire on the accelerator bar. He impounded the Corvette and had it towed to the barracks. He ordered the victim taken to a lab for an immediate autopsy. Anybody listening?"

"All Hicksville listens," Boyce said.

"A print man lifted one beautiful thumbprint in grease from that accelerator bar. Also, two more prints from inside the Corvette. A man's fingerprints, I add. Another lab man checked marks on the green paint, Corvette's hatchcover, and deduced it had been pushed by a car with a higher front fender. They took pictures, of course. They checked the Corvette's rear tires, exact widths, tire treads, etcetera. At the accident scene—no, opposite the Ford assembly plant—they checked the gunned marks Roy noticed on the concrete. The widths were identical to the Corvette's tires and the treads corresponded. They checked the soft shoulders and took moulages and pictures of the Corvette's tires where it had been parked. They did the same with a second car that had been parked directly behind the Corvette. We hope that second set of treads matches the club's Buick. Jim and I went over this material carefully. I told him we suspected the victim had not been killed in the crash, but had been murdered around eleven o'clock at Twin Springs. Freddy, cheer up. I liked the Hicksville ploy on Saturday. You got the idea from Jim Pelter in the Water Department, eh?"

"Yes."

"Now, Jim was with us. Generally, in an autopsy the medical examiner first cuts out the entire rib cage, so Jim phoned the lab and suggested he concentrate on the corpse's head. We took time out for a leisurely lunch of chicken sandwiches, a tossed salad, and excellent coffee. Then we joined the medical examiner. He explained about the corpse's badly battered face, that both arms were broken in several places, and that there were other external injuries. He had been surprised to find practically no external bleeding. Then he got Jim's phone call. He sawed off the top of the skull and extracted the brain. He found it virtually intact, with no bleeding, despite the terrific impact of the crash. Freddy, medical jargon is not my cup of coffee, but I remember that twice he said that the external battering occurred terminally. What did he mean?"

"By 'terminal,'" Raber answered, "he probably meant the point of death. Did he actually say Noonan had been dead before the crash?"

"Not at that point. What's the hoyoid bone?"

"It's hyoid, chief. I know generally."

"Okay, the jaw had been badly fractured. He became concerned about bruises on the throat might not have resulted from the crash. We watched him slice open the throat and expose the larynx. The hyoid is back— Freddy, can you take it?"

"It's a bone, often U-shaped," Raber explained slowly. "I'm remembering this from a strangulation case. It's positioned over the larynx, which is at the base of the tongue. Did the medical examiner say the hyoid had been fractured?"

"I think so."

"What was the blood condition at the point of fracture?"

"Ummm, I'm remembering 'fluid,' and I think he said dark."

"In court, chief, the murder will be death from asphyxia. An expert strangled Noornan and fractured the hyoid. The injury is lethal and death almost instantaneous."

"Freddy," Hocking enthused, "you often astound me. The ME said 'strangled' and 'lethal.' "

"Did he set an approximate time of death?"

"Hell, I didn't forget that! She probably died two or three hours before the crash at two o'clock. Now where are we?"

Boyce answered cheerfully: "We're in our jurisdiction—at Lodge Twelve, Twin Springs, at eleven o'clock on Friday night."

"Jim said it was our baby," Hocking added.

"How long will he sit on it?" Raber asked.

"Several days maybe," Hocking answered. "Now we need a motive for two murders and it's got to be a big motive, right?"

"I have something nebulous," Raber suggested.

"Spill it, Freddy. What have we got to lose?"

"We know," Raber began, "the employees do not know how to operate a private trout club. That suggests Twin Springs was purchased as a front for another enterprise that is highly profitable and illegal. We assume Noornan and Shellenbach found out about this illegality, but why or how those two did this can be shelved temporarily until we work out more important parts of the corpus delicti. The key point is that the employees had to shut the mouths of those two fast on Friday night, September seventh, between ten and eleven o'clock at Twin Springs. That suggests not only urgency, but a keen mind in control. The two murders were done silently and efficiently."

Raber glanced around.

"So far we've been lucky. We know the two murders were rigged to look like accidents. We also know the two murders are connected, although they occurred miles apart. Shellenbach's murder was simple, but Noornan's was complicated. I believe that was part of the plan to disassociate the murders. There was no identification on Noornan and that led the New York State Police to think she owned the Corvette and was the corpse. Wisely, they waited for a proper identification and Adele Myrick returned from Maine to provide that. Are we together?"

"Agreed," Hocking said impatiently. "What's the motive?"

"It has to be plenty of dirty money. Look at the facts we have, some of them apparently unrelated facts. Can we find any relevancy? John Barrington says Empire Export and Import are air freight expediters with headquarters in Jersey City and branch offices overseas. I believe him, but it's easy to check that out. Management brings in foreign fishermen who stay at the club only several days. How does that justify air fares from Shannon Airport, I believe, to Philadelphia and then home again? Fishing is a cover for their trips? With Big Ear, Roy overheard Joe Arragon ask the chef, 'Did you take your medicine?' Roy heard the chef answer, 'Not yet.' What do we have here, idle conversation or the clue to the illegality at Twin Springs?"

Raber was on his feet.

"In the drug racket, medicine means cocaine, the latest fad. In the basement at the farmhouse is a new room, two padlocks on the door. The outside hatch is kept locked. The entrance off Haycock Road is trapped at night and the chain-link fence is charged electrically. Those are innovations and very elaborate precautions. Why?"

Raber banged a fist against one palm.

"There's only one illegal business we know about where one dollar becomes ten or twenty dollars or more and that's the street sale of drugs. Roy, off your butt and get rolling."

Raber opened the door and strode off.

"Chief," Boyce drawled, "Fred's mind just pole-vaulted."

"Tonight, don't let Freddy go haywire," Hocking ordered, and Boyce nodded agreement.

That night they drew a zero at Twin Springs.

On Wednesday, September 12, Boyce drove to Jersey City. Raber visited the local office of the Bell Telephone Company, the Barrington home, and Sam Breadon, the electrical contractor. On Wednesday night they monitored Twin Springs and collected another zero.

"At least the repellent we used warded off the mosquitoes," Boyce observed cheerfully, and that summed up the situation.

14

On Thursday, September 13, Chief Hocking initiated a discreet surveillance by a squad car of the landing field at Twin Springs Trout Club to determine the answer to the question: When would Carl Krauthof and Paul Goodone return to home base?

At six forty-five P.M., Officer Ruthven telephoned headquarters. "I just witnessed the landing of the helicopter. Two men were aboard, husky Caucasians who fit the oral descriptions of the pilot and Goodone. They carried suitcases and entered the farmhouse." At seven thirty, when Boyce and Raber reported for their nightly stint with Big Ear, Officer Grace Gladwyn at the desk gave them this information.

Boyce said, "Now we should get some action," and sat facing Raber in the latter's small office.

"The weather holds warm," Raber noted. "For three consecutive nights, Arragon ate dinner with the chef, but Gene Palan dined alone on the screened porch. Will Goodone join him tonight?"

Raber let the question hang.

"Roy, the final autopsy reports on Noornan and Shellenbach confirm they died between ten and eleven o'clock on Friday night, September seventh. We must assume each one was alone when murdered and probably Shellenbach was killed first. Something must have broken fast between ten P.M. that demanded their lips to be sealed immediately, right?"

"That seems logical."

"As of now," Raber continued, "it's not of primary importance how the employees knew that Noornan and Shellenbach had learned about the illegal business. Shellenbach was an easy target. He was physically weak and I doubt he carried a weapon on a divorce case. About ten o'clock somebody visited him in Lodge One on a plausible excuse, knocked him unconscious suddenly and silently, then revived him in a tub of artesian water so he could inhale, and drowned him. Subsequently, he was eased into the pond. At Lodge Twelve, Evelyn Noornan was a more difficult problem. Prior to eleven P.M., she had to be unaware of Shellenbach's murder. Was she already in bed or still up? Was she preparing for bed? If she was dressed, what clothes was she wearing? Was she prepared to leave Lodge Twelve and dressed as the police found her in the wrecked Corvette? Roy, what do you assume and who handled her?"

"I'm assuming nothing, but I've been thinking about it. Palan had a pat story as to why Noornan left Lodge Twelve. I think he took Noornan alone. True, he's in his mid-fifties, but Dick Sprague noted he has big knuckles and thick wrists, both signs of power. She was athletic, so he had to take her unaware. Certainly Palan knew from the Corvette's registration that an Adele Myrick was the owner or he knew about Myrick from the permanent records in the office that John Barrington said always listed the name of the person to be called in case of an emergency. Okay, say I'm Palan. How do I take Noornan alone? Before eleven P.M. I knock quietly on the door at Lodge Twelve. Noornan lets me inside. I have a plausible story. The telephone line between the office and Lodge Twelve is temporarily out of order. So I had to take a phoned message for you. Make the caller a doctor at a New York City hospital—say Bellevue—but Palan would know a more appropriate one. Now, Adele Myrick had been in an auto accident and is asking for you. That readies you for a trip to the city. You are already dressed appropriately or you dress quickly. You are upset. It's easy for me to get close to you. I belt you in the solar plexus and knock you cold. Now, I must be aware of the hyoid bone. Let me change the pronoun! I strangle her, fracture the hyoid, and it's instant curtains for her. Wait—it's a warm night! Three hours elapsed between the death and the car crash. Wouldn't rigor mortis have set in rapidly?"

"True, but they could still wedge the body into the Corvette. I like your thinking."

Raber rose.

"That's enough conjecture, let's get with it."

Twenty minutes later they were in position across from the farmhouse, Boyce monitoring Big Ear.

"Fred," he whispered, "Krauthof, Arragon, and the chef are in the kitchen. Krauthof bellyached about the meal.... Ummm, Krauthof left, probably went upstairs.... Arragon to the chef: 'Did you take your medicine yet?' The chef: 'I always take it at bedtime.' A door closed in the kitchen. Maybe Arragon went outside. Can you see him?"

Raber stood up and peered at the farmhouse.

"I have him," he said softly. "He's wearing a white T-shirt. ... He walked up the lane past the barn. Do you have a fix on the others?"

Boyce beamed Big Ear further to his right.

"They're still at dinner on the screened porch.... Chitchat.... Wait, the chef arrived.... Palan ordered wine. Move it, Fred."

Raber backed from the bushes and edged to the side of Haycock Road. Wearing sneakers, he slipped silently across the macadam and crouched beside a stone pillar, the one north of the entrance. He remembered what Sam Breadon had told him in Suffern on Wednesday afternoon.

"I placed that photoelectric eye," Breadon had explained, "three feet off the ground and inside the pillar. If you work directly below the eye or on the opposite side of the pillar, you won't set off the alarm. The wires run from the eye to the ground and into a conduit to the farmhouse. Captain, you can snip those wires behind the pillar and that won't set off the bell inside the office."

Carefully, Raber reached around the pillar and found the wires. No bell rang inside the office.

Behind him pebbles click-clacked to a rolling stop on the macadam, Boyce's signal that nothing had changed inside the farmhouse.

Raber slipped to his right and paralleled the electrically

charged fence. He passed a stately maple tree outside the fence and advanced to a second maple, this one opposite the screened porch. He stood behind the pole and listened. He heard voices, but saw no one. Inside the wire screening of the porch was a lowered slat that leaked some light, but did not disclose who sat there. Dishes rattled.

They were now in the legal part of the surveillance plan.

Boyce would continue to man Big Ear, largely to protect Raber and create a diversion if that should become necessary. Without committing an act of trespass, it was Raber's responsibility to overhear whatever conversation took place between Palan and Goodone.

Directly over his head he eyed the lowest maple tree branch that jutted toward Haycock Road. He bent at the knees, leaped, and stretched his hands upward. At a height of eight feet, his hands closed around the limb. Momentum swung his body toward the farmhouse. He braked movement by placing his sneakers against the trunk and hoped he had made no sound.

He heard more dishes rattle and the sound of low voices.

He lifted his left leg and swung it over the limb, slowly elevating his body until he straddled the limb and sat facing the porch. What John Barrington had told him in confidence on Wednesday proved to be true—

"Captain, there's a strong limb that extends over that porch roof. I always meant to cut that limb off, but never got around to it. You see, in a strong wind that branch rubs the shingles and wears 'em. A maple limb is strong, too, and it will hold your weight easy. Hell, you do your job. I don't pry into police business, captain."

"Diego, that was an excellent dinner. The steak was broiled perfectly," Palan said clearly.

"Thank you, boss."

For Raber that settled two points. They were unaware of his nearness and Palan was number one at Twin Springs.

Grasping the maple trunk, he stood erect and climbed to the designated limb. Gripping it, he stretched his body along the top of the limb and held fast with one hand.

"These are good cigars," the chef said.

Goodone grunted. "Yeah, hold that light closer."

Raber now lay directly over the charged fence below and close to the porch. Between the end of the lowered slat and a post that supported the north extremity of the porch roof, he now saw a narrow gap, about four inches. Through this gap he spotted the edge of a table covered by a white cloth and a man's left arm. This seated man faced toward the maple tree.

"Diego," Palan said, "thanks for bringing the wine. You're through out here for the night. Clean up in the morning."

"Okay, boss."

Evidently the chef had left the porch, because Palan said, "We have to talk quietly out here, Paulo. Close that door. Diego likes to snoop and I don't want anybody to hear your report."

A chair scraped on a hard surface. There was no sound of a door being closed, but a chair scraped again. Raber now had the two men placed. It was Palan who faced the maple, and Goodone who was opposite him.

"Paulo, these are expensive cigars, my special brand."

"They're real good, boss."

Cigar smoke swirled through the gap. To Raber it was as if he sat at the table with the two men.

"Go over the business of air freight."

Goodone launched into a detailed report of overseas shipments by air to and from the Continent that seemed to prove business was steady and reasonably profitable. Here and there was some minor trouble, like a shipping clerk who had been fired, but the organization was smooth. To Raber, Goodone seemed to know the business thoroughly.

Palan concurred and as Goodone finished he said, "You're a top man, Paulo. My right arm. What about the other business?"

"We got no headaches there, boss."

"It took me over a year to set it up."

"Yeah, you worked hard."

"Thank you. It took brains with big money channeled overseas."

"You bet. Three banks used in Paris, boss."

"This next shipment—you followed instructions?"

"Right on the nose."

"Do you think sixteen K's is too big a batch to handle on one trip?"

"Naw."

"There will be the normal number of carriers?"

"Three flying Pan Am from Shannon to Philly."

"Their arrival time?"

"Sunday, ten thirty in the morning. The copter picks 'em up."

"Good. Who'd suspect trout fishermen?" Palan chuckled. "The stuff is safe in those false-bottomed tackle boxes and hollow rod handles."

"You got brains, boss."

"Exactly. And that's why I won't press our luck. This is the final here. Is the decoy trail set up?"

"They hired a French sailor on a tramp steamer, Marseilles to New York City. They only gave him half a K, but the dummy thinks it's bigger. A small loss. They'll tip somebody to pick him off."

For a long moment there was no sound.

"We're almost home free, Paulo. Counting the inventory total we have on hand here the total runs to three million dollars."

"Hey, the other three dummies know that figure?"

"I told them their cuts are against a half million dollars. You and I slice that big melon right down the middle."

"I drink to that, boss. How long do we sit on that wine bottle?"

"Ah, I'll do the honors."

In the stillness there sounded the gurgling of wine being decanted. Glasses tinkled together.

"Paulo, I propose a toast to two very smart men."

Pause.

"Boss, this is damn good wine."

"For us there is always the best. It's Château Lafite-Rothschild, 1961, a very good year."

There was a pause, then the sound of more gurgling.

"Boss, when we pullin' the hell outa this creepy woods?"

"We wait until the copter returns from Philly on Sunday.

Monday night, say at ten o'clock, we vanish completely in the copter."

"Everything set for that?"

"The other three don't know the time. We are packed and ready. In an emergency we can evacuate within seven or eight minutes."

Long pause.

"It's less than an hour's flying time to my farm on the island. Listen, Paulo, while my brain whirls. I'm finished with that sourmouth, Krauthof. Early on Tuesday we need him to ferry the copter back to the rental agency outside Trenton. You'll pick him up in the car I have at the farm. But why should we pay him fifty thousand dollars? Besides, in our new operation we won't need a pilot. My farm was once a potato farm and it's lonely. Hit him. Bury him in the woods out there and you earn his fifty thousand, right?"

"It's a deal, boss. Hey, I been using the head, too. You want to waste twenty-five grand per on Diego and Arragon?"

"No. You shut their mouths and we'll make this a two-man operation. And you pick up their shares, also."

"It's done, boss. We split the three million down the middle. Hey, we split the last of that wine, too?"

There were sounds of more wine being poured.

All so casual, Raber thought, as if they were swatting flies.

A car hummed along Haycock Road, then rushed off. In his cramped position atop the limb, Raber stirred.

Then, off to his left, inside the charged fence and close to the farmhouse, a shadow advanced. It wore a white T-shirt.

Below Raber, Joe Arragon arrived silently outside the screened porch and stood immobile. If he glanced upward—

"We've touched all the bases, Paulo."

Somebody yawned.

"Jeez, I'm beat. Boss, I'm gonna hit the sack."

"You've worked hard. You deserve a long, long rest."

"Is everything else in place?"

"You mean locally?"

"Sure."

"It's very peaceful and quiet, thanks to my planning. Oppenheim, my lawyer, picked a perfect location. The police are not too bright, so there's no worry in that direction. The other areas are also quiet. Paulo, we pulled it off."

Chairs scraped across a hard surface.

Raber glanced below. Arragon was already a retreating shadow and Raber thought, The poor guy arrived a trifle late.

A door opened and closed. On the porch a light winked off.

Raber climbed silently downward. With his sneakers planted solidly on a branch, he began to exercise first one numbed leg and then the other. He studied the front side of the farmhouse. Arragon had left.

Raber grabbed the lowest branch with both hands and lowered himself to the ground. Behind him on Haycock Road he heard the mounting sound of an approaching car. A long light shafted ahead under the trees. He placed the maple trunk between himself and the light. The car gunned past, its lights outlining the fence, the gateposts, the office, and there stood Arragon. The car sped off.

Raber slid around the tree so that it was between himself and Arragon. On the fence side, he peeked out. Over the door into the office, a night light glowed and moths fluttered about the bulb. Arragon advanced to the entrance, pausing before reaching the pillars. Light glanced off metal in his right hand.

He went inside for a gun, Raber thought.

Arragon lifted his right hand. Suddenly, strong light lanced out and illuminated the run of chain-link fence that ran to the outlet brook. The light swung in a 180-degree arc and stabbed along the fence next to Raber. He glued himself to the tree. The light winked off. Raber waited thirty seconds, then peeked around the tree. A small stone landed on the macadam and rolled to a stop near the tree.

Boyce's signal for all clear. There had been no real danger. Arragon was city-trained and out of his element.

It was time to head for home and pull in the chief.

15

IT WAS ten fifty, Thursday night.

With the door to the chief's office closed, they finished coffee and remained grouped around the desk with Laird Hocking in his swivel chair and Roy Boyce and Fred Raber on either side.

"Chief," Raber suggested, "before we dig into it finally, why not let Roy see the enlargements of those pictures?"

"I'm sorry, I thought he'd seen them," Hocking said and handed Raber a manila envelope from his drawer.

As Raber opened the envelope, he said in explanation, "We figured there was a roll of undeveloped film in the Leica camera we confiscated at Lodge One and we also wanted to know what pictures Shellenbach had snapped on the case he was working. We sent the reel of color film to Ardnor and later the chief checked the developed pictures. A number were of Mrs. Lorning and Werner DeHaven in somewhat compromising situations on the porch of Lodge Two. The chief mailed those, plus the negatives, to Mrs. Lorning with a brief explanation. He ordered enlargements of six other pictures. A squad car picked them up this afternoon and that's what we want you to see."

He handed Boyce an enlargement.

"For the first time, meet Evelyn Noornan."

Boyce studied a color photo of a smiling, dark-haired, evenly tanned, tall woman poised atop the dam near the spillway at Twin Springs. She wore a wet yellow bikini and carried a white bathing cap in one hand. Drops of water sparkled on her body.

"This is top photography and Shellenbach knew his business," Boyce mused. "Man, she's lovely."

"Tut, tut, you're to be married in November," Hocking reproved.

"That fact doesn't impair my vision." Boyce laid the picture on the desk. "They're callous bastards to destroy such loveliness."

Raber arranged five enlargements atop the desk.

"Why Shellenbach photographed the employees individually, we don't know, but he went to a lot of trouble. He snapped them from a bedroom window in Lodge One with the screen removed. The background is the lane above the barn. The light angles are dissimilar and that suggests different times and even different days. Meet the gang."

Boyce studied each picture in turn, then asked, "Chief, do you have a large reading glass handy?"

Hocking produced one from his desk and handed it to Boyce, who adjusted it over the picture of Gene Palan.

"How old do we figure him?"

"In the mid-fifties," Raber answered.

"Magnification reveals no age lines or wrinkles in his face. Hmm, the mustache is quite black, no gray hairs. The head hair is luxurious and black, but why the touches of gray? I think he's wearing a wig. Is that a disguise to make him look older?"

Hocking used the glass and confirmed, "It's a wig. On a trifle crooked," and passed the glass to Raber, who said after an intensive study, "There *is* gray in the wig. Shave off the mustache, take off the wig, and we may have a man who is forty years old."

He returned the glass to Hocking.

"Chief, Palan's bare arms show plenty of muscle and he may move quickly. If he took Noornan, she had no chance."

Raber collected the pictures, slid them into the envelope, and dropped it on the desk.

"Chief, will you make the summarization?"

"First," Hocking said, "my congratulations to both of you. Since Freddy has direct oral evidence, we forget Big Ear existed. Drugs is their illegal racket. It's pure stuff, possibly heroin, smuggled through Customs in false bottoms in tackle boxes, hollowed handles on fishing rods, and so on. The carriers are real fishermen or dupes. We can't be critical of Customs. They have an impossible job with too little money appropriated, too few inspectors, too many points of entry, and thousands of passengers arriving daily on planes. This operation represents big money. Empire has the money for the buys overseas, to pay all the handlers, to lay false trails, to handle the packaging and the other details. Twin Springs is the local cover and that new room in the basement of the farmhouse may be the cutting center. They have accumulated a huge inventory that may be ready for street sale and huge profits. The operation is about to end with this final shipment of sixteen K's. We know a K equals 2.2 pounds, about eleven pounds per carrier for the three fishermen who are to leave Shannon Airport Sunday morning early, September sixteenth, on a Pan Am plane. The arrival time at International Airport in Philadelphia is ten thirty. Now, Palan plans to double-cross three employees and we believe he gives Goodone the same treatment. Neither of you overheard any mention of Harry Shellenbach and Evelyn Noornan, but we can write that into the script. To us, the drug angle is secondary. We want that gang for two first-degree murders. They plan to pull out completely, after dark, Monday, September seventeenth. They board the copter, head for Palan's farm less than an hour's flying time distant. We agree that mention of an island, an old potato field, and the short flying time pinpoints that farm as being on Long Island. Out there, Goodone murders Krauthof, the chef, and Arragon and collects their cuts, fifty thousand dollars. He buries the bodies in the farm's woods, right?"

Raber nodded and Boyce said, "Excellent summary, chief."

"What we now have," Hocking resumed, "is limited breathing space. We hatch plans and catch them with the drugs in their possession, then stick them with two murders. Freddy?"

"I'd like to give it a lot more thought, chief."

"Sure, sure, and we're all tired. What are the main lines of our approach, eh?"

"On Saturday, you and I go before a county judge. I present the evidence and we obtain a search warrant for Twin Springs, nine P.M., Saturday, September fifteenth. We hit the farmhouse with a small raiding party and have reserves nearby. We sweep all five employees into our big basket, plus the evidence."

"Do we still play it Hicksville?" Boyce asked.

"You bet, kiddo."

Hocking decided, "We'll work out the kinks tomorrow morning and start the show on the road," and they headed for home.

16

It was Saturday night, September 15.

Inside a squad car with only the parking lights showing, three members of the raiding party waited for a legal entry into the premises of the Twin Springs Trout Club.

Wearing soft clothes and no hat, Fred Raber sat behind the wheel with his car parked south of the bridge over the outlet brook. To his right sat Officer Rose Scafide. In addition to the clothes the women wore while on desk duty, she sported a blue-white hat and a smart blue jacket with a white armpatch blue-lettered FHPD. She was unarmed. On her lap lay a manila envelope. Lieutenant Sprague, in full uniform with a .38 in a shoulder harness, sat on the rear seat.

Raber noted the time, eight fifty-five, on his wristwatch.

Large, drifting clouds intermittently blanked out the stars and a waning moon. The weather had turned much colder and that precluded anyone from dining on the screened porch.

"For the benefit of Rose," Raber said casually, "I'll review the procedure. We hit the farmhouse exactly at nine o'clock with a search warrant. Dick explained the downstairs floor plan and we proceed accordingly. We expect to find the front office door locked. We park by the south end of the farmhouse and enter by the kitchen door. Roy Boyce will have his .357 Magnum out. He and Dick handle the employees in the kitchen. Rose follows me along a central hallway to a doorway, probably closed, on the left into Gene Palan's living quarters. We enter and I serve the warrant on Palan, the boss. Now, we expect no real problem, Rose. We play it Hicksville. Rose tabulates the illegal evidence we obtain. However, you are to react intelligently to any unforeseen development. We herd all employees into Palan's quarters. Dick takes Goodone into the basement. If the padlocks are set on that new room, he blasts in with his .38. We have a backup on Haycock Road. If I fail to phone headquarters at nine twenty, the backup sirens move in."

"Clear, captain," Scafide said, and Sprague drawled, "Ditto."

"We have two minutes," Raber said, and watched the road ahead.

Thirty seconds edged past.

Up ahead by the bridge a red light winked twice.

"The situation is go," Raber said. "All the employees are inside."

He switched off the parking lights, started the engine, and drove forward. At the bridge Boyce appeared and Raber braked the car. Boyce joined Sprague on the rear seat.

"I snipped the wires on the electric eye," he reported. "No alarm bell rang inside. Fred, I know the whereabouts of all five employees. Two in the kitchen, Goodone with Palan, and Krauthof upstairs. I ditched the wire cutters and you-know-what at our hiding place. Rose, is the adrenalin pumping fast?"

"Angel face, I'm ready to yawn."

It was thirty seconds before nine.

Raber drove forward, eased the squad car left through the entrance pillars, and let it coast past the office door with its overhead lighted bulb. He braked at the end of the farmhouse, cut the engine, and slid the keys under the front seat. They left the car quietly, Raber leading the way. He passed a lighted, curtained kitchen window and reached the door. Gently, he twisted the doorknob and pushed in. The door was unlocked. He nodded to Boyce, who had his Magnum out. Raber went in fast. Joe Arragon lounged opposite a central table. Diego Ramose wheeled from a position by a refrigerator.

"Don't move, this is a police raid," Raber warned softly.

"Play it cool," Boyce hissed, and swiveled the Magnum.

The two men froze.

"Is the stairway into the basement trapped?" Sprague whispered to Arragon.

Arragon shook his head.

Sprague stepped outside. Seconds later he returned and said, "Fred, it's quiet out there," and left the door ajar.

With Scafide at his heels, Raber crossed the kitchen and entered a dimly lighted central hallway. Toward the end of the hallway and on the left the door into Palan's quarters stood closed. Raber opened the door and shouldered inside. In this spacious lighted room, Gene Palan sat behind a large desk with dinner dishes for two on its top. Paul Goodone lounged nearby and started to rise. Palan waved at him to remain seated.

"This is a police raid," Raber snapped. "The guns are coming right in, see? I'm Captain Raber, local police. Palan, this is a legal raid. I have a search warrant—read it and weep."

He tossed the official document on the desk.

"What's the reason for this nonsense?" Palan asked politely.

"We got a tip, a letter in the mail. You guys run a drug racket out here. Read the document, Palan."

"I accept your word, captain," Palan murmured. "But what flimsy evidence—a letter in the mail. In a court of law my lawyers will tear that warrant into legal shreds and I will hold you legally and financially responsible for this intrusion into the privacy of—"

"Shuddup!" Raber interrupted.

Arragon and Ramose entered, followed by Sprague, who had his .38 out. Boyce appeared, rubbing his hands together.

"Lieutenant," Raber ordered, "take Goodone into the basement. If he don't unlock that new room down there, blast off the locks."

"Move it, buster," Sprague said, and Goodone rose and started from the room, Sprague at his back.

"Hey!" Boyce exclaimed. "I count only to four!"

"You are a mathematical genius," Palan murmured pleasantly.

"Only four guys, captain. Where's cabbagehead?"

"To whom does this lad refer?" Palan asked.

"He means Krauthof, the copter pilot. Where is he?"

"Why, upstairs in his bedroom. May I summon Mr. Krauthof over our small intercom system?"

"But don't pull any funny stuff," Raber agreed.

"Most certainly not, captain."

Palan pressed a button on a small console.

"Carl, do you hear me?" he asked quietly.

There was a grunted response.

"Carl, we have visitors in my office. Please join us immediately."

"Okay, boss."

"Did you tip him off?" Raber demanded.

"Why, captain, I respect the authority of the police." Palan smiled. "What's your next step in this silly charade?"

"We search this place top to bottom and find the drugs. If I don't phone headquarters by nine twenty, a backup crew sirens in."

"That's very clever, captain."

"Rose," Raber ordered, "out with the steno pad and pencil. Write down all the items we confiscate. In five minutes we—"

"The door, the door!" Scafide warned.

Raber wheeled.

Carl Krauthof had arrived. He carried a short-barreled shotgun and pointed it at Raber.

"All visitors freeze," Krauthof growled. "I got six shells in the pump and I can't miss at this range."

"Just a second!" Raber sputtered. "Palan, that search warrant is legal! A judge issued that warrant and behind him stands the whole state of New Jersey!"

"You are a jackass," Palan said.

He opened a desk drawer, dipped in his right hand, which emerged with a gun.

"Jackass, the shotgun and this .38 say fornicate your search warrant and your judge and New Jersey." Palan's manner became authoritative. "Diego, get a clothesline from the kitchen."

The chef hurried from the room.

"Joe," Palan ordered, "search that young dummy from the rear."

Arragon patted Boyce down.

"Boss, no gun on him now. In the kitchen—"

"Search the captain," Palan interrupted.

As Arragon passed behind the desk, Raber groaned, "Jeez, I left my gun at headquarters."

"How thoughtful," Palan said. "Joe, search him."

From the rear, Arragon patted Raber down.

"He has no gun, like he said, boss."

Ramose returned with a coiled clothesline.

"Cut the rope into lengths six feet long," Palan ordered briskly. "We'll truss them to chairs like dummies."

"Please don't search me!" Scafide squeaked. "I don't have a gun!"

"Ah, despite the fact that you are somewhat attractive," Palan drawled, "you must be tied." He laid the .38 atop the desk. "That's a lesson, my dear, not to keep such bad company."

Standing near the desk and using a sharp spring-bladed knife, Ramose sliced the clothesline into lengths.

Palan strolled over to Krauthof.

"I'll keep them covered," he said, and took the proffered shotgun, which he handled expertly. "Carl, tie that young man. Diego, work on the captain. Work from the rear of the chairs so that I have a clear shot. Joe, handle the woman."

"I don't want to sit on a straight chair!" Scafide sobbed. "Can I sit behind the desk, please?"

"Very well," Palan agreed.

Two employees began to tie Raber's and Boyce's arms and legs to chairs. Arragon conducted Scafide to the easy chair behind the desk where she continued to cry softly.

"I won't hurt you," Arragon soothed.

"I'm—I'm scared!"

"You won't get away with this! I'll follow you!" Raber raged.

"In your crude language, shuddup," Palan advised. "If you can sprout wings you can follow our helicopter."

Goodone strode into the room, carrying a .38 which he laid beside Palan's gun on the desk.

"I took that stupe's gun, boss. He's tied and gagged."

"Good work, Paulo. Listen, everybody. We follow our regular plan to evacuate in an emergency. I'll remain on guard. Let's move it."

The four employees hurried from the room.

"Our deadline is nine twenty. We still have eleven minutes," Palan said and crossed the room to a closet.

Shifting the shotgun to his left hand, he opened the door, leaned inside, and brought out a large, expensive-looking suitcase. He closed the door, carried the suitcase to the main door, set it on the rug, and returned to a position alongside the desk.

"Captain, I am about to further demonstrate my superior intelligence. We'll be long gone before your backup squad arrives. Now, watch what I do, but you won't be able to solve the puzzle."

Palan faced a sectional bookcase against a far wall beyond the foot of a single bed. As he strolled forward, Rose Scafide waved both hands at Raber. In her left hand she held a pair of scissors and in her right one of the .38's. Raber shook his head.

Ahead of Palan the top section of the bookcase swung open.

"How clever I am," he said as he dipped his free hand behind the closed section. "And look what I have discovered!" He withdrew an attaché case which he settled under his left elbow, then reached inside again.

Frantically, Rose Scafide signaled to Raber.

In answer, his lips framed an emphatic word, "No," and in disappointment she laid the .38 and scissors on the desk and placed her arms behind the chair as if she were still tied.

Palan faced around. In his left hand he carried the shotgun and in his right two attaché cases. As he strolled back to the desk, the open section of the bookcase swung slowly and noiselessly into its original position. Placing the cases atop the desk, he repeated his performance at the closet door and emerged with a second suitcase. He carried it across the room, set it beside the other one, turned, and smiled at Raber.

"I assume your salary is roughly ten thousand dollars a year. If you totaled that sum for forty years, it would still be short of the cash I have in these two attaché cases. Behold the reward, captain, for superior brains."

"It's dirty money," Raber sneered.

Goodone returned and arranged four packages by Palan's suitcases. Each was encased with a shiny black material, sealed with tape, and tied with cord. Drops of water adhered to the wrapping.

"I got all four," Goodone grunted.

"There is the evidence you sought," Palan explained, "but you would never have found it."

"You hid them in the pond, right?" Raber snapped.

Palan laughed.

"Okay, you hid them in the outlet brook!"

"Captain, your score is zero."

The other employees began to return. The chef placed a cheap fiber suitcase with the other luggage, plus a large filled brown sack. Arragon added a suitcase and a rectangular package. Lastly, Krauthof lugged in two heavy suitcases.

"We are way ahead of schedule," Palan announced pleasantly. "Later, I shall reward each of you suitably. We shall not leave in a group."

Goodone stepped to Palan and whispered urgently. Palan nodded and turned to Raber.

"I offer a final puzzle in this little game, captain. What does this mean? It is Kennedy Airport, tomorrow afternoon at two o'clock, and three passengers arrive together. A man meets them and tells them to wait with their luggage until he returns with a car. He leaves and—"

"Cut the crap!" Raber growled. "By God, you won't get away with this! You'll all end up in jail!"

Palan smiled.

"Carl, you leave with Paulo and warm up the helicopter's engine."

Palan handed the shotgun to Goodone, who picked up the three black-wrapped packages. Krauthof grabbed two suitcases and the two men left. A minute passed.

"Diego," Palan ordered, and the chef took his suitcase, the paper bag, and the rectangular package, which seemed light, and left alone.

Palan eyed his wristwatch casually. Another minute passed, after which he said, "Joe, take everything else."

The big man hefted the remaining luggage easily and waited.

"It was nice to meet such cooperative visitors," Palan said, and pocketing his .38, picked up the two attaché cases. "Good night, everybody." Palan bowed from the hips. "I'm really sorry to leave you in such uncomfortable positions."

Arragon followed him from the room. Ten seconds passed.

Scafide stood and picked up Sprague's .38.

"We can still take them!" she whispered.

"Use the scissors," Raber suggested, "and cut Roy loose."

She laid the gun down, picked up the scissors, and cut Boyce's bonds.

"Thanks," Boyce said, and stood and stretched.

Rose Scafide took three steps toward Raber.

"Rose," Boyce drawled, and she wheeled.

In his right hand, Boyce held a .357 Magnum.

"My God!" she gasped. "I—I—Joe searched you!"

"Cut the captain loose. I wonder if he has his Magnum?"

Seconds later, Raber was freed and stood.

"Rose is a big girl," Boyce said and chuckled. "Fred?"

"It's really quite simple," Raber explained. "On a man, one area is rarely frisked and certainly not by an amateur like Arragon."

Raber opened his jacket.

"We're both wearing athletic supporters over jockey shorts. We could have taken them at any moment before we were tied up."

He slid a hand down inside the front of his trousers. "We used the supporters as holsters." His hand emerged with a short-barreled Magnum. "Rose, you did a nice con job on Arragon and he tied you so you worked free easily."

"Hello, dummies," a male voice said, and they turned to the far wall where Officer Montanez stood between parted drapes at an open door. He wore a baseball cap, dark clothes, and sneakers. In his right hand he held a .38.

"What's this?" Rose Scafide asked.

"I was with Roy when he cut the wires at the front entrance," Montanez explained. "He pegged Krauthof alone upstairs. So I climbed a maple tree to the porch roof and entered through an unlocked window." Montanez smiled. "When Krauthof left his bedroom with a shotgun, I tailed him downstairs in case the party got rough. It didn't and I circled to this spot to watch the proceedings."

"Well, well," a new voice said, and they turned to the door into the nearby corridor. "Why aren't you dummies tied to chairs?"

"Major John Orwell, head of the County Investigative Staff," Raber said. "Where's Lieutenant Sprague?"

Carrying a walkie-talkie, Orwell entered the room.

"Freddy, I'm sorry that I slipped up. I entered the kitchen when it cleared and sneaked down to the basement. I found their lab room was unlocked and stripped. I waited behind a pillar until Sprague brought Goodone down, according to the plan. Damn, Goodone moved fast. He pulled a gun from inside his belt and clipped Sprague behind the ear. He tied and gagged him. That's all or I'd have taken him with my gun. As soon as the last two employees cleared the farmhouse, Sprague and I came upstairs and I pulled in a cowboy with this walkie-talkie. He said he was all right, but he's got a lump behind one ear. The cowboy drove him to the hospital for X rays."

"I knew it, I knew it!" Scafide exclaimed.

"She's Rose Scafide, a probationary officer," Raber said. "She's very smart and cool under fire, major. She freed herself early and wasn't in on the master plan."

"Rose, what was it you knew?" Orwell asked politely.

"Sir, I knew the captain wouldn't let them walk out free. Besides, I listened and listened!"

"Ah, you're repetitive. You listened for what?"

"The sound of the helicopter engine starting up. It makes such a racket! When it didn't start, I knew, I—"

She broke off laughing.

"Major," Raber suggested, "will you fill Rose in and bring all of us up to date?"

"Rose, out here it was the captain's scheme," Orwell began. "It's a simple ruse that deer hunters use. One group moves in behind the deer and sets up a racket. As they advance, the deer take off downwind and run into the other hunters, who have guns. The ruse is called spooking and it's unfair to use it against city men. Freddy, where had they hidden the drug inventory?"

"They were in waterproof packages in the breeding pools, major. What we might not have found was Palan's bankroll in two attaché cases which he bragged contained close to a half million dollars."

"I figured out the gimmick on that one," Boyce confessed, and opened the door into the closet. He reached inside. "I've got it, it's a switch." Starting at the desk, Boyce faced the bookcase and advanced slowly. The top section swung out noiselessly. "The closet switch activates a photoelectric eye and I passed through the beam." Boyce flashed his cherubic smile. "Palan had his cash hidden in there."

"Nice going, Roy," Orwell said and turned to Scafide. "My dear, would you like to hear the rest of it?"

"Please."

"You're in a nice rut tonight. This is a big operation, about thirty operatives involved. Chief Hocking is in charge at the Municipal Building where we have a temporary headquarters and the building is sealed off. We have three FBI agents because of the interstate and overseas angles to the case. Here we have several local officers who know the territory. The rest of the force are Treasury agents, some here with the guns and others at headquarters for the paperwork. In charge is Lance Davis, Treasury Department, and some of his men were pulled in from as far away as Boston. The five employees were caught with the goods on them. They were covered from the rear of the farmhouse to the helicopter, which had been rendered nonoperative by an expert. Oh, no employee tried to skip out on his own. In the barn, their Buick and jeep were also nonoperative. We had a guard on the road around the pond and one at the dam to prevent any access to a guest's car and to keep the guests in their lodges. Haycock Road is also blocked. It was a tight trap, Rose. All five men are in custody, not one shot fired. That's what we call perfect teamwork."

Orwell turned to Boyce.

"Roy, I've arranged for you to stay at the farmhouse. Mr. Davis has some technicians coming in to collect evidentiary materials. They were very careless in that laboratory in the basement. I had time to check. There is discarded broken equipment in two trash baskets. I wet a finger and rubbed it on equipment here and there. Acid, man. We'll nail them good."

Orwell eyed Montanez.

"Your captain tells me you're a crack shot with a .38."

"Thank you, sir." Montanez smiled. "I had our people covered and they were in no real danger."

Orwell took Rose Scafide by an elbow and steered her toward the door into the corridor.

"My dear," he began, "I'm always alert to recruit smart, cool officers. Give this a thought. The county offers a high wage scale, an excellent pension system, and—"

They entered the corridor.

"Monty," Raber said, "thanks for your good work. See that the lieutenant gets his gun back. It was in the plan for him to get taken downstairs, but not that realistically."

Raber shook Boyce's hand.

"Goodnight, Hicksville. Maybe you can learn something from the experts in the Treasury Department."

"Hell, I can only count up to four, remember?" Boyce laughed. "Now comes the tough part, nailing that gang for two brutal murders."

Raber nodded.

17

AT POLICE headquarters in Fair Hills, at ten fifty-five P.M., Saturday, Officer Gladwyn manned the desk. With her in uniform were Sande Nosse, on special assignment, and Rose Scafide, who had been bubbling the news of the successful raid at Twin Springs. By the door of the chief's darkened office Major Orwell and Fred Raber stood in quiet conversation.

"Any change in the interrogation plans, Freddy?"

"Not at present," Raber answered.

"At the outset, Mr. Davis agrees. I expect no difficulty as his men are very busy. The haul is much bigger than anybody anticipated. Oh—your boss plays a shrewd hand of poker."

"Which means, major?"

"Before we first met with Mr. Davis, it was Laird's idea to withhold the idea that our primary interest in the case was not drugs, but first-degree murders. Smart, because that charge supersedes drug conspiracy. Thus, we have the five employees next door, not whisked off to Newark. All set, Freddy?"

"Any time."

"Switch on the intercom between your office and this one. I want to keep abreast of developments."

Orwell addressed the three female officers.

"Girls, whoever is free, join me. Interrogation of a prisoner is an art. Your captain, of course, is an expert." Orwell smiled easily. "Besides, no show of uniformed officers in here. That is *Miranda* versus *Arizona*, United States Supreme Court, June, 1966. As an interrogation progresses, I'll explain more Miranda. What's my luck?"

Free at the moment, Nosse and Scafide entered the chief's office. Orwell followed, leaving the door ajar and the lights off.

Raber stepped to the desk and handed Gladwyn his jacket and gun.

"I don't want to run afoul of the Supreme Court in the Miranda case," he explained. "During interrogation, an open gun suggests force."

"During the past week," she said quietly, "there's been considerable unexplained activity around here. I asked Sergeant Parisi what was up and he almost snapped my head off."

"What did he tell you?"

"That he was in the dark, too. He said a good officer kept the eyes and ears open and the mouth shut."

"That's sound advice, officer. So?"

"Things are breaking open tonight. I did hear on Friday about an autopsy report, but told nobody. Captain, do we have a murder in Fair Hills?"

"No, Grace. We have two murders."

The corridor door swung open and Raber turned. A stocky man in civilian clothes stood there with the chef.

"Where do I find Captain Raber, please?" the man asked.

"You're speaking to him."

"I am Robert Burns, Treasury Department," he clipped off. "I have been instructed to deliver the prisoner, Diego Ramose, into your direct custody and do so now."

"Thank you, Mr. Burns."

Burns glanced around and asked, "Do you have security here?"

"Yes, full security."

"You guarantee this prisoner will be returned to our custody?"

"I do. Has the prisoner been thoroughly searched for weapons?"

"Yes, sir."

"Diego," Raber directed, "please sit on a chair by the wall."

The chef sat on a straight chair.

"Cross the right leg at the ankle, please."

The chef obeyed the instruction.

Raber walked forward and said, "Mr. Burns, this is rather unorthodox procedure, but—"

In fluid movements, Raber jerked a brown loafer off the chef's right foot, felt inside, withdrew an object, and dropped the loafer onto the lap of the surprised chef.

"One spring-bladed knife," Raber noted and pressed a button on the bone handle. "This has a thin sharp blade designed to penetrate a victim's heart whether he's stabbed from the right or the rear." Raber shook his head. "You're a naughty boy, Diego." Raber closed the knife and handed it to Burns. "Take this weapon with you."

Silently, Burns hurried from headquarters.

"Stop looking so surprised, Diego. In Mr. Palan's office you got some rope and pulled that knife from your right loafer to cut lengths. Afterward you rehid that knife."

"Yeah, I think nobody seen me!"

"Mr. Ramose," Gladwyn advised, "it's just as easy to say 'yes' as 'yeah.' Also remember you are addressing a police captain."

"Yeah—uh, yes!"

"No more tricks, Diego," Raber suggested, and pointed to the open door into his lighted office. "Step in there."

Raber followed Diego and closed the door.

"Diego, take the chair alongside the desk."

"Yes, captain."

Seated behind the desk, Raber switched on the overhead mike that funneled sound into the chief's office.

"Diego, what is that machine atop my desk?"

"It is—one tape recorder, yes."

"The recorder is not turned on yet. Before you were turned over to me, you were in the custody of the United States Treasury Department. You are in trouble with them, right?"

"Yes, captain!"

"We shall see how deep that trouble is and that depends on your answers to some important questions. You understand you are now in the custody of the Fair Hills Police Department?"

"Yes, captain."

"Don't push the captain bit any further. And relax." Raber smiled. "Do you know why you are here?"

142

"No."

"I'll explain the situation."

Raber handed a large color photograph to the chef.

"Who snapped that picture of you?"

"I don't know."

"When was it snapped?"

"I don't know."

Raber took the picture from the chef and turned it over.

"Diego, during the past week, you and the rest of the employees at Twin Springs must have been asleep when you were supposed to be awake. It says on the back of this picture that you entered the United States from Puerto Rico nine years ago. While you were operating your own diner in New York City, it says here you were arrested for pushing drugs. You were convicted on that charge and spent two years in prison with time off for good conduct. Diego, is that correct?"

"Yes."

"Pushing drugs was a stupid mistake?"

"I was one big fool!"

"You were a fool to carry a switchblade knife around. That knife is illegal and you know it. Shall I forget about that knife?"

"Please, please!"

"It's forgotten. From now on I'm going to call Palan by his right name. How long have you known Gino Paladino?"

"A few months is all."

"How old is Paladino?"

"Maybe forty, I'm not sure."

"Is his black mustache real?"

"Sure, he grows it."

"Did Paladino wear a wig?"

"Captain, you notice! Sure, he wears a wig."

"To make him look older?" Raber prompted.

"Yes. Also it is a disguise."

"When did you first meet Paladino?"

"That is—February. Yes, this year."

"You went to him?"

"No, no. He sends a messenger. I go to his home, Park Avenue."

"He is a bachelor and lives in a five-room apartment?"

"Hah, you know everything!"

Thanks in part to the T-men, Raber thought, and said aloud, "Tell me about your first conversation."

"He don't say how he knows about me. He offers me a job, good wages. I cook for him. I keep his apartment neat, too."

"You have a wife and a small son in New York City?"

"Yes."

"When you were hired, did Paladino know you had a prison record?"

"Yes. He says that don't matter to him."

"When did you learn about coming to Twin Springs?"

"That is—last week in March, yes."

"You arrived in Fair Hills on April first. It was a bigger job?"

"Sure, I get bigger pay."

"Later you learned about the drug operation. At Twin Springs, in any way, did you ever handle any drugs?"

"No, no! I kiss the cross and say no!"

"To keep your mouth shut about the drugs, did Paladino promise to pay you the sum of twenty-five thousand dollars?"

"Mother of God, you know all!"

"You were to be paid at Paladino's farm on Long Island?"

"Yes!"

"After you arrived there on Monday night?"

"Yes!"

Raber leaned back in his chair.

"Diego," he said quietly, "by having you arrested tonight, I saved your life. If you had reached Paladino's Long Island farm on Monday night, he would not have paid you twenty-five thousand dollars. And you would never have seen your family again. Let me prove that. On Thursday night you served broiled steak to Paladino and Goodone on the screened porch. Afterward, you even lit Goodone's cigar. Did you bring them a bottle of choice Château Lafite-Rothschild wine?"

"Y-yes!"

"When Paladino told you that you were through for the night, you left the porch door open. Goodone closed that door so you couldn't hear what they talked about. But *I* heard what they talked about."

Raber paused. He is smart, Raber thought, and adapts quickly to a changing situation. And he is all yours. Raber closed in.

"Diego, I heard Paladino tell Goodone to kill you for your twenty-five thousand dollars and Goodone agreed to bury you on that farm."

"No, no!" the chef protested, coming up off the chair. "It is—they don't do that to me!"

"Sit down, Diego."

The chef collapsed onto the chair.

"Why, why?" he asked brokenly. "I am little man!"

"But you know too much and not just about the drugs. You know about the two murders."

"Y-you know t-that!"

"Calm down, Diego. I want you to think."

The chef took a deep breath.

"Now you know why you are here. Those two murders occurred in Fair Hills and it's my job to solve them. I want your help. I want to know who killed Harry Shellenbach. I want to know who killed Evelyn Noornan. If you had nothing to do with those two murders, I may be able to help you. Think, Diego. Ask yourself what you owe Gino Paladino. He owes you twenty-five thousand dollars and he didn't intend to pay you. He planned to double-cross you. He planned to kill you and—"

"Stop, stop!" the chef pleaded. "You tell me this—what for?"

"Because I want you to tell the truth. Did you kill Harry Shellenbach or have any part in his murder?"

"No, I swear it!"

"Shellenbach was drowned in a tub inside Lodge One. Later, his body was placed in the pond. You had a part in that?"

"Merciful God, no!"

"Evelyn Noornan was murdered in or near Lodge Twelve that same night. Did you have any part in her murder?"
"No!"
"Of your own knowledge, not hearsay, do you know who murdered Harry Shellenbach and Evelyn Noornan?"
"Hah, I know about that man!"
"Will you tell me about Harry Shellenbach?"
"Sure, I don't kill that man!"
"It is your decision to talk?"
"Sure!"

Raber started the tape recorder.

"This is a recording in Police Headquarters, the Borough of Fair Hills, New Jersey, between Captain Fred Raber and Diego Ramose. Mr. Ramose is a chef, now employed by Empire Export and Import Company, the owners of Twin Springs Trout Club. The time is eleven three P.M., September fifteenth. The subject is the first-degree murder of Harry Shellenbach, a private detective, in residence as a guest, Lodge One, Friday, September seventh. Mr. Ramose, are you ready to talk?"
"Sure."
"Are you handcuffed?"
"No."
"Is any physical force being used against you?"
"No."
"Do you sense any force being directed against your person?"
"No."
"How long have you been in my office?"
"A few minutes, captain."
"Mr. Ramose, you have certain legal rights. You have the right to remain silent. If you volunteer to talk, what you say may be used against you in a court of law. You are entitled to make one phone call. Mr. Ramose, do you wish to make a phone call?"
"No."
"What you are about to say is offered voluntarily?"
"I want to talk, yes."

"You are entitled to the services of a lawyer. If you lack money to hire a lawyer, the state will provide you with a lawyer free of charge. Mr. Ramose, do you wish the services of a lawyer?"

"No."

"As you tell your story, I may interrupt to ask a question. I won't try to change any fact in your story or change your story. You say what you have to say. Any question I ask will be to make clearer what you wish to say. Mr. Ramose, you understand?"

"Sure."

"Start with the events of Friday night, September seventh. Tell where you were and what you were doing."

"It is six o'clock and I am working in my kitchen. The guests catch trout and I broil trout for them. Joe Arragon he delivers. It is six thirty and Mr. Shellenbach he comes in my kitchen. He has a trout and says deliver it to Lodge One, eight o'clock. He gives me a two-dollar tip. I broil his trout. I deliver it on the dot, eight o'clock. That's in Lodge One, only a short ways."

"You saw Harry Shellenbach alive at eight o'clock?"

"Damn right, alive! In his kitchen, Lodge One. I am busy, busy—more broiled trout. Joe Arragon he delivers. I cook dinner for Goodone and Gino Paladino and serve 'em on the screen porch. I cook for Joe Arragon and Carl Krauthof. They eat in my kitchen. Nine o'clock, Joe he leaves. He likes the country and takes walks at nights. Carl, he goes to his room upstairs. I work, work, eat, and clean up. Ten o'clock, Carl he comes in. I ask where he goes. He says maybe that dame she undresses with the lights on and—"

"Wait," Raber interrupted. "Who is the dame?"

"Miss Noornan, Lodge Twelve, very close. Carl, he watches her before and she undresses with the lights on. She is stacked, we say! I finish work and go outside. I sit by the trout pools and cut dough to feed 'em. That's for ten-twelve minutes maybe. Carl, he sneaks down from Lodge Twelve and I ask why the rush. He says he listens under a bedroom window and hears Miss Noornan and Shellenbach talking in bed. They know all about the drugs. She leaves at eleven o'clock and drives home to New York. Next day is Saturday and she tells the cops about all the drugs. Carl, he goes inside and I follow. I am much worried! I see him knock on Gino Paladino's door downstairs. He goes in and I listen outside. I hear Carl tell them what he tells me. Paladino is the boss and he says he will take care of it and—"

"Wait," Raber said. "By them, you mean Goodone and Paladino?"

"Sure. Look, I don't want to get caught listenin'! I run to my kitchen and start to make fresh coffee. I hear Carl go upstairs, no rug on the steps, see? It's ten twenty and in comes Paladino and—"

Raber interrupted: "Why are you so sure of the time?"

"I worry, worry, and watch that 'lectric clock over the refrigerator! Paladino asks do I still save coins and wrap 'em. I say sure and he asks have I got one of nickels. I say sure and he says go get it. I live upstairs in the barn. I hurry there and put on the light by the Buick and jeep. I go up and get a nickel wrap and come down and there is Paladino waiting."

"You mean a wrap around nickels," Raber suggested, "not a nickel wrap. How many nickels were inside the wrap?"

"Always twenty! He puts the wrap in a pants pocket and—"

"No," Raber said. "Tell it exactly as you saw it. Into which pocket did Paladino put the nickels?"

Ramose took a deep breath.

"Captain, Paladino carries a bottle of wine in his left hand. It is Château Lafite-Rothschild, very expensive. So Paladino takes the wrap of nickels in his right hand and shoves it into his right pants pocket! He says I am through work and I climb the stairs and he puts out the light. I worry, worry! I make noise closing the door, but I don't go in. I take off the shoes and sneak down and run to windows at the back of the barn. It is bright out, the moon shining! I see Paladino walk up the lane and on the dam and he is gone behind—no, he is in front of Lodge One! I run from the barn and go up the lane. Jeez, stones hurt my feet! No shoes on the feet, see? I walk on the grass a cat up to the dam. Nobody is on the porch. I sneak close and hear voices inside and—"

"Diego, were the windows at the front of Lodge One open?"

"Sure."

"Were lights on inside the main roon?"

"One light, easy to see inside. Can I talk more?"

"Go right ahead."

"Mr. Shellenbach, he stands by the table in the big room. He wears shorts, tan color. Later he has on—"

"Not yet, Diego. Position Paladino. In which hand is the bottle of wine? Keep his hands clear exactly as you see it."

"Hah, I see it! I see the backside of Paladino. The wine bottle is in his left hand. His right hand is inside his right pants pocket. Paladino tells Mr. Shellenbach the wine is a gift, it just came in by the copter. That is a lie, always that wine in cases in a closet in the kitchen! Mr. Shellenbach reaches for the bottle. He don't see Paladino bring his right hand out from his right pants pocket. *Bam!* Paladino belts him in the belly. Mr. Shellenbach's eyes pop and he drops to the floor. No sound from him after that *Bam!* The boss sets the wine bottle on the table. He sets something else there. It's that nickel wrap he had inside his fist. Paladino stands over Mr. Shellenbach. He pulls off the tan shorts. Under the shorts is jockey shorts, yes. He pulls them off and the sneakers, too. Mr. Shellenbach is bare-ass. Paladino carries those clothes into the front bedroom. He comes out and he has in his hands red swim pants like Mr. Shellenbach always wears. Mr. Shellenbach, he is out cold. The boss puts the red swim pants on Mr. Shellenbach and drags him into the john. A light comes on in the john. It is quiet and I hear water start to run, splash, splash. I wait, maybe it's two minutes. Hah, I hear more water run? No, the splash, splash is over!"

"What did you do next?"

"I run like hell back to the barn!"

Raber stopped the tape recorder. He thought for a moment, then pressed a button on the recorder and waited until the story had been erased.

"Diego, thank you very much. I want you to tell your story a second time exactly as you saw it happen. This time I shall not interrupt. A stenographer will take your story down in shorthand. She will type it and you will read it. Then you may sign it. Officer Nosse, please."

A moment later she entered, carrying a notebook and pencil, and sat down in one corner.

"Mr. Ramose, meet Officer Nosse," Raber said.

They nodded to each other and smiled.

"Officer," Raber said, "after Mr. Ramose completes his story, double space the transcription and make a carbon. Place the original in a folder and take it to Chief Hocking in the main building. He understands Mr. Ramose must initial each page and he will witness Mr. Ramose's signature at the end and attend to the other details. Mr. Ramose, I must repeat to the officer the time, place, subject, and so on."

Raber outlined the background to Nosse, who wrote steadily.

"Sande, add this. Mr. Ramose, we must review your legal rights. Do not hurry your answers. Do you make this statement willingly?"

"Sure, I want to get it off my chest."

Raber outlined the rights of the witness and received answers.

"Sande, you understand there may be no typographical errors on the original of the deposition?"

"Yes, sir."

"Diego, tell your story."

He talked and there were no interruptions.

At the conclusion, Raber rose and said, "Diego, this way."

In the main room Raber turned Ramose over to Officer Gladwyn, who conducted him off. Orwell strolled from the chief's office.

"Freddy, the prosecutor will love this. We have a rarity in a first-degree murder, practically an eyewitness."

"Do you think he can stand up under a tough cross-examination?"

"He's no dummy and his story has the ring of authenticity. I liked his use of the present tense, as if he were reliving the events. Oh—Joe Arragon should be along in a moment."

"For that we can thank your diplomacy," Raber said, and the major entered the chief's darkened office.

Gladwyn returned.

"Captain, I caught most of it. It was fascinating."

"It was brutally fascinating," Raber said, and waited, his left elbow propped on the high desk.

18

AT THE door into Police Headquarters, a black man asked, "You are Captain Raber?"

"I am, sir."

"Officer Maylor, Treasury Department. I now deliver into your personal custody this prisoner, Joseph Arragon."

"I accept delivery."

Arragon wore a white T-shirt, tight blue jeans, and sneakers. He stood awkwardly, his hands behind his back.

"I plan to interrogate," Raber said. "Please remove the handcuffs."

"That's a condition of the Miranda ruling," Maylor observed. He stepped behind Arragon, unlocked the cuffs, and stepped away. "Sir, he is a very powerful man."

"Yes, he is."

"If the justices of the Supreme Court worked at our level, captain, their rulings might be different," Maylor added and left.

"Hello, Joe," Raber said.

"Good evening, captain," Arragon said softly. "Thank you for the favor. I dislike wearing cuffs."

"There are times when that's necessary."

On cue, Officer Rose Scafide breezed in from the chief's office, advanced to Arragon, and smiled up at him.

"Joe, I had hoped to meet you again. Golly, you're big!"

"Thank you."

"No, it's the other way around. I thank you. Earlier at Twin Springs you treated me very gently."

"You were upset. I didn't want to hurt you."

"Joe, please bend down."

He did.

She lifted on tiptoes and kissed him on one cheek. As he straightened, red stained his face and she laughed softly.

"Joe, you're in trouble. Listen to me, please. I'm your friend. Captain Raber is your friend. We both want to help you. Please, will you trust us?"

Arragon hesitated.

On her way out Scafide said quietly, "Joe, believe in us."

Raber gestured toward his office. "Sit by the desk, Joe."

He followed Arragon inside, closed the door, sat down, and switched on the overhead mike.

"Joe, you were born and raised in New York City?"

"Yes, captain."

"You liked the country life at Twin Springs?"

"Yes."

"And you took long walks alone at night?"

"Yes, and on my day off, too."

"Why?"

"It's quiet there," he said softly. "The air is clean. I like that pretty officer. What is her name?"

"Rose Scafide."

Arragon moved his wide shoulders, a ripple of latent power.

"She reminds me of another woman. I met her at the club and she was very nice to me."

"Who would that be?"

"Evelyn Noornan. She was a guest in Lodge Twelve."

"When did you first meet her?"

"It was the Fourth of July week. I took trash from the lodge. She talked to me, like she was interested."

Raber waited, and Arragon added, "That was the time Miss Noornan gave me a little book."

"What kind of a book?"

"Well, I told her this was my first time in the country and I liked it. She said she was raised on a farm. In Michigan, I remember. She gave me the little book to keep. It had colored pictures of birds and things about them. She said find the birds in the book. I mean I was to match the book birds with the ones at the club. She was coming back for ten days in September. She said we'd take walks together. She'd know then how many birds I matched."

"Any luck, Joe?"

"She said good. I knew robins, bluebirds, catbirds, song sparrows, all easy. Over the pond, I knew tree swallows and barn swallows. They fly graceful. I matched chimney swifts, too." He sat relaxed, his big hands folded on his lap. "I like wood thrushes best. They sing at dusk, always two notes. You know that church bell that rings the hours?"

"Yes, it's on the Baptist Church."

"That's the way a wood thrush sings, sweet and clear like a bell. Why did you want to see me?"

Raber drew a colored photograph from a drawer and handed it to Arragon. "Did you know somebody snapped your picture at the club?"

"No."

"Have you any idea who snapped this picture?"

"No."

Raber took the picture back but did not glance at the information on the reverse side.

"Joe, you were eighteen years old. You worked for a small firm of movers. The police caught you and your boss removing furniture from a house. Your boss was sentenced eight-to-ten years in state's prison. You were given a one-to-two. What's the story?"

"That boss said he had a contract to move the furniture." Arragon shrugged. "I behaved myself in stir and got out early."

"That means you have a record."

Raber placed the photograph in the drawer.

"We'll start with Thursday night, this week. You went for a walk and then you sneaked along the front of the farmhouse. You wore a white T-shirt. You stood by the screened porch where Paladino and Goodone sat. Why were you there?"

"I don't trust them."

"I was very close to you, Joe."

"Sure, I saw you."

"Beg pardon?"

"You lay on a tree branch over my head. So close maybe I could jump up and touch you."

Raber stared in disbelief. "How'd you happen to spot me?"

"I guess it's this bird thing, captain. Birds are small and I learn to see everything. There was some light from the porch and you are bigger than birds. It was funny, you trying to hide."

"Why didn't you sound an alarm?"

"I figured you don't trust them two."

"Joe, like you and I played on the same team?"

"Maybe."

"You were right not to trust them. Just before you arrived, they made plans to handle you."

"I know. Goodone is to kill me on Paladino's farm on Long Island. It was Paladino's idea and he is no good."

Arragon opened his hands with the palms uppermost.

"On Long Island I plan to kill Paladino. With these hands tight on his throat."

"Do you know what an IQ test is?"

"Sure, I took one in stir. I scored big. One hundred, captain," he added with a touch of pride.

The seconds ticked past. The big man had knocked Raber off balance and Raber knew it was unwise to push ahead too fast. The idea was to keep the prisoner talking voluntarily and to switch tactics, if necessary, to regain control.

"Joe, are you hungry?"

"I can always eat."

This was Miranda again. A prisoner who is being interrogated has the right to relaxation periods and food.

"What kind of sandwiches do you like?"

"No more tuna. The chef, he liked tuna. Captain, he fed me tuna till it come out of my ears."

"Right. What about coffee?"

"Sure."

"How do you like it?"

"Always black, just one sugar."

"Your order is coming right up." Raber stretched. "At Twin Springs, were you ever in that new room in the basement?"

"No."

"Did you ever handle the drugs, even to package them?"

"No. Paladino did all that work."

"After stir, you did a number of odd jobs. The last one was

at a Turkish bath on West Forty-eighth Street in New York City. Was that where you first met Gino Paladino?"

"Yes, four-five times."

"Did he offer you a job?"

"Yes. In a freight warehouse. I took the job in January."

"Did Paladino know you had a prison record?"

"Sure, he knew all about me."

"At Twin Springs, when did you learn about the drugs?"

"That was the last of April. I tried to quit. Paladino said I can't, it's my prison record. An ex-con in one state can't go to another state. I quit the job and he has to turn me in. Back I go to prison. I stayed."

"Paladino lied to you, Joe. You served your time and were free to go anywhere. To New Jersey, Illinois, even to California."

"My hands are full!" Scafide called in.

Arragon moved quickly and opened the door.

"Thanks, pal Joe," Scafide said, and entered carrying a plate of sandwiches and coffee. "No tuna fish," she added and set the dishes on the desk. "Are you and the captain friends?"

"Sure, we play on the same team."

"Captain, would you like something?" she asked.

"Yes, but it's not food."

"Joe, if you want seconds, just speak up," Scafide said, and she left, closing the door.

Arragon began to eat. Raber went back over it.

"Thanks, captain. The coffee was good," Arragon said.

"Would you like a second cup?"

"No. Uh—could I go to the john?"

Miranda had popped up again.

"Follow me," Raber said and they walked through headquarters, into the adjacent corridor, and around a corner where Raber indicated a door marked GENTLEMEN.

"Joe, you're on your own."

The moment Arragon disappeared into the lavatory, two uniformed officers eased around a nearby corner. One was Crawford, a local man, and the other a county patrolman.

"Captain, isn't that big man a prisoner?" Crawford asked.

"He is, Pete."

"You're not wearing a gun."

"I don't need a gun."

"Suppose he tries to climb out a window?" the county man asked.

"He won't, he's quite docile."

"Are you putting me on?"

"No. In his spare time the prisoner studies birds."

"You *are* putting me on!"

"Sssh," Raber warned. "He's coming out."

The officers hurried out of sight as Arragon walked out. They returned to Raber's office. He chose to move straight ahead.

"Joe, on that Long Island farm, you planned to kill Gino Paladino. That was because he had murdered your friend Evelyn Noornan?"

"Yes."

"When did you plan to kill him?"

"On Tuesday morning."

"Why did you pick that time?"

"Carl Krauthof is to fly the copter back to Trenton that morning. Goodone is to leave early in a car to pick Carl up. The chef is nobody and it's me and Paladino. He has a full belly from breakfast. I grab his throat and choke him slow. Carl told me about that farm and the woods. I bury Paladino in that woods. I put big stones and logs and leaves on his grave. Paladino has all his cash in the house in two cases. I take my twenty-five grand. The chef takes his."

Raber prompted: "Then?"

"A mile away is a wide highway to New York City. Carl told me he followed that in the copter to reach the farm. We wait at a gas station. I give a truck driver twenty dollars and we hitch a ride to the city. Diego, he goes home to his wife and son."

"Weren't you afraid Goodone would follow and kill you?"

"No, captain. Maybe he finds Diego, not me."

"Why wouldn't he find you?"

"In the country you double back on the trail. That's like a

deer does, captain, and I read that in a book at the club. At the end of Haycock Road is a river and a house with a sign. It says rooms to rent and I stay there. Nobody looks here for me."

"When were you sure Paladino killed Miss Noornan?"

"For sure, on Sunday."

"But you knew on Saturday, the day before, she was not in Lodge Twelve?"

"Diego told me she drove home to New York City on Friday night."

"Do you know when Miss Noornan was murdered?"

"Sure."

"Tell me about it."

"Well, Mr. Shellenbach and Miss Noornan, they are very good friends. I think they are in love. She is gone from Lodge Twelve and I worry about her. Saturday afternoon I follow Diego to his room in the barn. I stand over him and he is a little mouse. I said talk and he talks. He said Paladino killed Miss Noornan behind Lodge Twelve on Friday night. About eleven o'clock, Carl told him. I told Diego not to tell anybody he told me. I waited. The city is all rush, rush. In the country there is no hurry. Paladino can't run away. On Sunday Carl and Goodone fly off in the chopper. Paladino ate lunch on that screen porch. I warn Diego to stay in his kitchen. I go right up to Paladino and ask why he killed Miss Noornan. With his own lips he said he had to kill her. She found out about the drugs and she drives to New York Friday night to tell the cops the next day about the drugs and we all end in jail. I told Paladino how smart he is to save us. I asked how did he kill her and he told me with his own lips. He had Carl fix the Corvette so it can't start. He heard the starter whine and no engine noise and he went there. He told her Carl would fix the engine to start. She got out of the car and stood up. He had a roll of nickels in his right fist. He slugged her on the jaw and broke it. Captain, he laughed. He said she can't scream with a broken jaw. He told me he is so clever and she is on the ground. He choked her and killed my friend. He left my friend alone on the ground. I told him he is real smart. Wait—Carl told me about the car accident on Route

Seventeen. I do not know cars, but Carl does. He made it look like an accident with the Corvette, him and Goodone. Diego told me that Paladino had drowned Shellenbach in a tub. I thanked Paladino for that. So I wait. I listen. I work. I hear. We three know too much, and that Paladino is crazy. I fix him on Tuesday morning at his farm. That what you wanted to know, captain?"

"Thank you, Joe. Let me think out loud for a moment."

Raber sat quietly.

"These are important notations, Rose. Notify the New York State Police to use a centrifuge on the victim's clothes and the front seat of the Corvette. On Sunday morning, send Boyce to the parking lot behind Lodge Twelve. Major, can you dispatch a technician and a centrifuge with Boyce? The parking lot is unpaved. The victim lay there for some two hours and we need corroboration of that fact. Also, check the front bumper of their Buick for green paint samples and check that against the green paint on the tonneau of the Corvette. Rose, I need you. Joe, thank you for waiting."

"Sure. I'm alone, I talk to the squirrels."

"Do the squirrels ever talk back?"

"They chatter, chatter. They whisk their tails and run up trees."

Officer Scafide entered with a notebook.

"Rose, who has the desk tomorrow?"

"Lieutenant Waslewski, sir."

"Type the information you just heard over the mike in triplicate. One for the major, one for Waslewski, one for the chief, but do that after you type Joe's story with a carbon. The original, we hope, is headed for the courts. Officer Nosse will tell you how to proceed after you have Joe's story typed with no errors."

Scafide sat and crossed her legs. She laid an open notebook across a thigh, poised a pencil, and waited. Raber dubbed in the background details. Next, he covered Arragon's legal rights and received answers.

"Joe, tell your story to Rose. Tell it in your own words to the best of your knowledge. Start on Saturday when Diego told you that Gino Paladino had drowned Harry Shellenbach in a tub inside Lodge One. Also that Miss Noornan was no longer in Lodge Twelve on Saturday morning. I suggest you omit what you planned to do to Gino Paladino on Tuesday morning at his farm. However, that is your decision, but remember that you were only thinking and never carried out your plan. Joe, you are on your own. Just think out loud."

Arragon began to talk, softly and slowly and steadily, with no break in his story and with no mention of his plans for Gino Paladino.

"Joe, you did very well," Raber approved, and he rose and left the office to join Officer Gladwyn. "Please take Joe back to Mr. Davis," he said, and joined Orwell in the chief's darkened office.

"The case is shaping up solidly for the county prosecutor," Orwell decided. "Once, while Joe was talking, Rose started to cry and I told her police only cry when they're alone and off duty."

He stood and switched on a desk lamp. From an inner jacket he drew out a sheaf of thin documents and held them in his right hand, like cards in a poker hand.

"These are arrest warrants for first-degree murder," he explained. "There is one for each employee, just in case Mr. Davis decides not to cooperate. However, I understand he is still very busy." Orwell dropped two warrants on the desk. "We won't need the ones for Ramose and Arragon, as they seem to be in the clear." He returned the other three warrants to an inner jacket pocket. "Freddy, I picked up two items of interest. A preliminary check of the contents of Paladino's two attaché cases shows he carried over four hundred thousand dollars in big bills. Those four waterproofed cartons contained drugs ready for street sale and the belief is the stuff is all heroin. I know this. It's by far the biggest drug haul ever made in this country. Freddy, stay in there."

Orwell hurried off.

19

IN THE business of interrogation, Raber had learned from experience there was never a set line of approach because individuals differed so enormously. Techniques that succeeded with a Ramose or an Arragon would not work with a Carl Krauthof or a Paul Goodone. As a general rule, with no prompting from *Miranda* v. *Arizona,* ruses or tricks were self-defeating. A duped prisoner turned into a clam. On the other hand, frankness often succeeded for the same reason that the superior hand in a poker game captured all the chips in the pot. Strong facts such as "This we know and can prove in court" often convinced a suspect that to lie or to clam up or to evade simply exposed his weak position.

Major Orwell strode in.

"Freddy, I had to show Mr. Davis an arrest warrant to get Krauthof here. He thought we were intruding into the drug conspiracy, but he's sympathetic now that he knows we're interested in solving two murders. It's after eleven thirty. Can you speed it up?"

"I'll try," Raber said, "but Krauthof holds the key."

Orwell went into the chief's office and switched off the desk light.

Officer Burns entered with Krauthof. Earlier, Burns had been stung with Ramose and the switchblade knife. Now he said, "Captain, I deliver Carl Krauthof into your custody," and left.

The prisoner wore a soiled white shirt open at the neck, rumpled brown slacks, and dirty sneakers. Wide through the shoulders, he weighed an easy hundred eighty pounds. He stood silent, arms locked across his chest, glaring at Raber.

"Copper, what's this all about?"

"You are thinking—"

Krauthof interrupted: "You're no mind reader."

"I'll give it a try. You think, 'I'll walk over this little cop and run free.' Would you care to try?"

"Yeah, I will."

The door into the rear area swung open. In full uniform, but minus a cap, Officer Montanez emerged and drew a .38 from a shoulder rig in a practiced move. He set his right elbow atop the high desk, leveled the gun, and squinted along the barrel.

"Mr. Krauthof," he said softly, "note that the gun is aimed at an empty office. An officer points a gun at a man when he is prepared to shoot. At thirty yards I can place a bullet into any part of your body I choose. Would you care for a demonstration?"

"You're a dumb pig," Krauthof sneered.

"No, I'm a trained police officer."

"Here's the book on him," Raber said. "He has a sour disposition and an acid stomach. There is a—"

"Very funny, copper!"

"—contract out on him, Monty. For fifty thousand dollars, which is far more than his hide's worth."

"Very funny!"

"Ah, note how lightly he dismisses a hit."

"Why the hell bring me in here?" Krauthof demanded.

"Monty," Raber said, "his surname means cabbagehead. That big knob on his shoulders either contains a brain or is only good for cole slaw."

"Very funny, copper. You're a stand-up comic."

Raber pointed to his lighted office.

"Go in there and sit beside the desk."

"I don't have to!"

"There are many things you don't have to do, cabbagehead. You don't have to go to the john. You can wee in your pants."

"This jerk is a helicopter pilot," Montanez drawled. "With his brain, captain, how does he become airborne?"

"Perhaps he flies by the seat of his pants."

Officer Gladwyn snickered. "Not him," she offered. "His pants are too soaked with wee-wee."

Krauthof stormed into the office, slammed a chair against

the wall, and sat down. Raber followed, closing the door. He switched on the overhead mike.

"You do not have to answer this question," he began pleasantly. "In the other room, were you fingerprinted?"

Krauthof hesitated. "Yeah. So what?"

"That saves us sixty seconds of your valuable time."

Raber had decided not to show Krauthof a color photograph of himself, nor to divulge, at the moment, the man's military record, which the FBI had provided. He drew three stiff papers from his desk, selected one, and laid it before Krauthof.

"That is a thumbprint from a man's right hand. Do you notice any unusual marking on it?"

"No."

"Then you must be blind. When you enter the cabin of a helicopter, do you grope your way?"

"Okay, it has a scar!"

"You're doing better, but you don't have to do this. Place your right thumb uppermost alongside that thumbprint."

"Go to hell!"

"That is a brilliant answer. I'll try once more. There is a contract out on you for fifty thousand dollars, or your share of the drug racket at Twin Springs. From Paladino's farm on Long Island, on Tuesday morning you were to return the rented helicopter to Trenton. Then, Goodone was to kill you for your share. Well?"

"That's a lie, copper!"

"I have no reason to lie. Refusing to compare your thumb to the print is your privilege. Why refuse? You know that thumbprint is yours."

Raber paused reflectively.

"I believe you should have asked where we lifted that print."

"Screw you!"

"We lifted that print from a new green Corvette. The owner is an Adele Myrick, London Terrace Apartments, New York City. She is a cotenant of Evelyn Noornan, who you know was a guest in Lodge Twelve at Twin Springs. We lifted that thumbprint from a film of grease on the extension of the accelerator bar under the Corvette's hood. You wired the bar down so the throttle was almost open. You—"

Krauthof interrupted: "That ain't so!"

"Don't try to con me. That thumbprint proves you were on Route Seventeen before two A.M. last Saturday. You had to work fast on a delicate job. You wore no gloves. We lifted two more of your prints from inside the Corvette. As you planned, the Corvette crashed at high speed. You murdered Evelyn Noornan."

There was a sudden change in Krauthof.

"Captain," he pleaded, "you gotta listen! Sure, I rigged the Corv to crash, but I don't kill that dame! That dame was dead before the crash!"

Raber laughed contemptuously.

"Cabbagehead, you listen to me and don't interrupt. You will be on trial for the first-degree murder of Evelyn Noornan. We will introduce a picture of that beautiful woman before the crash. We will introduce a picture of her battered face after the crash. We will introduce your three prints taken from that Corvette. We will introduce a picture of the wired-down extension of the accelerator bar. Technicians will corroborate these facts. On your day in court, where does that leave you?"

"I—I—she—she was already dead!"

"You think a jury will believe that? It's—too—late—for you. The jury knows it. Your attorney knows it. You know it. You're holding the bag for the first-degree murder of Evelyn Noornan."

"I'll talk!"

"You now want to tell your story voluntarily?"

"Damn right. I don't hold the bag for Paladino!"

"Begin at nine P.M., Friday, September seventh. After you had dinner in the kitchen, why did you leave the farmhouse and where did you go? Be exact as to the times if you know the exact times. If an employee tells you what he did, try to remember what he said and repeat it."

Krauthof talked. Raber inserted questions for the purpose of clarification.

"Captain," Krauthof finished, "that's the God's honest truth!"

"Will you repeat your story to a police stenographer?"

"Yes."

"Afterward, you will have a chance to read the typed statement. If you agree with that statement, will you sign it?"

"Sure, I don't kill that dame."

Raber said, "Officer Nosse, please," and a moment later she entered and sat down. Raber did not introduce her to Krauthof.

"Sande," Raber said, "disregard the detailment of this man's military record which the FBI provided. Mr. Krauthof, you enlisted in the army and flew choppers in Nam. You faced a court-martial for selling drugs to military personnel, but were found not guilty. However, you were permitted to resign, you received a dishonorable discharge, and you were returned to the States. Afterward, when you applied for jobs as a commercial pilot of helicopters, what happened?"

"I don't get hired. That damn discharge!"

"When did you first meet Gino Paladino?"

"That was in—yeah, March, this year."

"Did he know about your dishonorable discharge?"

"Captain, he give me a break!"

"Sande, we'll start the deposition. The same instructions apply as for the deposition of Diego Ramose. Mr. Krauthof, this statement is voluntary on your part?"

"Yes."

"These are your legal rights." Raber read from a form. "Mr. Krauthof, do you wish the services of a lawyer?"

"No."

"Tell your story."

"I come down to the kitchen at Twin Springs. It was about ten o'clock Friday night. Uh—that was September seventh. I had time on my hands and maybe Evelyn Noornan undressed with the lights on like I seen her before. Diego asked where I'm headed and I told him. I sneaked up to Lodge Twelve. It was dark in her bedroom and the open windows are right above my head. I heard some talk. She was in bed with Harry Shellenbach and they was goin' at it. I know their voices. Pretty soon she asked for a cig and a match flared. They talked and they knew about the drugs in the basement. That's in the farmhouse. She said plans had changed. Tonight at eleven o'clock she drives the Corv to New York City. The next morning she runs to the law and spills the story. Shellenbach is to sit tight in Lodge One. I sneaked down to the farmhouse. Diego sits by the trout pools and he asked what's up and I told him. I hurried in to Paladino because I had fifty grand riding on this. Paladino and Goodone are downstairs and I told 'em what I heard. Paladino said go to my room and wait for orders. Before eleven o'clock Paladino sneaked in and asked could I fix the Corv so it don't start. I said sure and he said fix it. That was no problem. I removed the distributor. Back at the farmhouse I met Paladino and asked about Shellenbach. He said, 'I drowned him, you stay with Goodone downstairs.' So I wait with Goodone and asked him about Shellenbach and he said, 'The boss drowned that rat.' Eight after eleven o'clock Paladino come back. I got that time from my wristwatch. It's a good watch, I bought it cheap in Nam. Paladino said, 'I fixed her good.' I kept the mouth shut. Paladino said go to my room and wait for orders. He come in at one thirty by my watch. I heard Arragon, he snores. We sneaked downstairs and up to the Corv. Goodone is there and so is the dame. Paladino whispered to put the dame in the front seat, but not behind the wheel. She is flat on the ground next to the wheel. I bend down and her jaw is all crooked. I picked her up and she is stiff. I got her into the Corv. Paladino covered her with a blanket. We can't start the Corv there, too much racket. I put the distributor back. Next, it was one hell of a job! They pushed. I pushed and wrestled with the wheel. You see, the Corv had power steering and the engine ain't running. We backed out the Corv on the parking lot and shoved it to the lane and I slid behind the wheel. It's downhill and I wrestled that Corv to Haycock Road. We shoved it north and went back to the barn. We rolled out the Buick and lined it behind the Corv. Man, we was all sweatin'.

Paladino left. Goodone give me a roll of fine wire and we went over how I was to wire down the accelerator bar. That dame is already stiff-dead. Paladino killed her and I'm off the hook for murder, right?"

"Mr. Krauthof, I suggest you omit the last part. That is a conclusion," Raber said quietly.

Krauthof hesitated. "It's the truth."

"That is not the point. The jury draws the conclusions after they hear technical testimony. Believe me, tell it as it is."

"How do I get that stuff out?"

"Instruct the officer to cross it out."

"Pretty officer," Krauthof said, "cross out that stuff."

Without looking at him Nosse drew lines and waited.

"Go on," Raber prompted.

"So, I drove the Corv and Goodone trailed in the Buick. There was no traffic north on Route Seventeen. I parked the Corv on the shoulder near that car assembly plant. Goodone is right behind. I lifted the Corv's hood and went to work with the wire on the accelerator bar. I know my business and it took me maybe two minutes. One car passed, but it don't stop. I got the hood back in place. There is no blanket on the corpse. Goodone's got it in the Buick. I don't try to move the corpse. Now, it's teamwork and we're good with cars. Goodone nudged the Buick against the Corv. I had the window lowered and reached in and turned on the ignition key. The engine sputtered and roared. That throttle is three-quarters open, see? I close the door and grab the wheel with my right—no, my left hand and wave the right hand to Goodone. He inched up the Buick's speed and we got the Corv straight on the concrete. Now it's real tricky. I wave to Goodone. He upped the speed to seven-eight miles. I'm running, see? I reach in with the right arm and slip the Corv into high gear and he gunned the Buick. Christ, that Corv took off like a jet! I boarded the Buick and rolled down a window to watch. The Corv runs straight and gains speed, all lights on. *Wham! Crash! Bang!*—like it's Fourth of July. Goodone swung left through a gap in the divider fence and got the hell outa there. We told Paladino it's rigged like an accident. I'm tired. I went to bed and slept."

"Thanks, Sande," Raber said and she left.

Krauthof wiped sweat from his face with one hand. Raber rose and beckoned Krauthof to follow. At the desk, he told Officer Gladwyn, "Take him to Mr. Davis."

"Hey, I'm free of a murder rap?" Krauthof demanded.

"You are a cold-blooded bastard and you desecrated a corpse," Raber said contemptuously, and joined Major Orwell.

"Freddy, that was a nice sign-off from a nonswearing man. I note the developing pattern in those three employees. They all have records for Paladino to hold over them. What about Paul Goodone?"

"We'd better work on him as a team," Raber decided.

20

PAUL GOODONE stood inside the door of headquarters.
He had cropped black hair and no expression in his dark eyes or on his face with its olive cast. He was muscular in a hundred-eighty-pound frame. A short-sleeved blue shirt open at the neck revealed a hairy upper chest and thick arms. He radiated an air of belligerence as he stood flatfooted, his fists at his sides.

"Mr. Goodone, you'd better forget any idea of escaping," Raber warned pleasantly.

"You an' a black bitch," Goodone grunted and slid his left foot forward and cocked his right fist.

Simultaneously Officer Montanez erupted from the rear area. He did not draw his .38, but stood alertly behind the high desk. Officer Gladwyn grabbed a nightstick and hurried along the desk. Major Orwell, carrying a gun, loomed in the doorway of the chief's darkened office. Raber waited, his feet spread, his hands open at belt level and his eyes on Goodone's cocked fist.

Goodone drove a high right at Raber's unprotected jaw. Raber flicked his head aside and the fist passed over his left shoulder. For a second they stood chest to chest. Raber used his open hands to push Goodone backward, then drove a solid left into Goodone's body, the knuckles landing below the rib cage. A right followed the left. Air whooshed from Goodone's lungs, and he started to sag at the middle as Raber turned away.

"Honey," Raber said, "he won't call you another name."

"Freddy," Orwell applauded, "I've heard you were very good. Thanks for the demonstration. Officer Gladwyn, we'll restore order in here. A cup of water, please."

Orwell rolled Goodone over on his back.

"He's out cold."

Montanez chuckled. "I've boxed with the captain, but he never hit me *that* hard. Captain, that was beautiful."

Gladwyn handed Orwell a cup of water from a cooler.

"I'll drown him," Orwell announced, and doused the man's face.

Goodone stirred, then opened his eyes. Orwell heaved him to his feet and stood him against a wall.

"Mr. Goodone, listen carefully. I am Major Orwell, head of the county police. I saw you attack an officer of the law. Captain Raber knocked you cold with his fist. Do you understand?"

Goodone stood silent.

"It is customary in such a circumstance," Orwell continued, "for the prisoner to charge police brutality. You're bigger and stronger than Captain Raber. Do you wish to prefer charges?"

Goodone remained impassive.

Orwell pointed to Raber's office. "Sit beside the desk and wait."

Goodone reeled into the office and Orwell closed the door. "Freddy?"

"The FBI said he's an ex-soldier of the Mafia," Raber explained. "He has an arrest record as long as his arm. He has one conviction, an A and B, and drew two years. When he left stir, the Mafia didn't pick up its option. For five years he's been Gino Paladino's strongarm. Major, shall we give him a whipsaw?"

"I'd be delighted."

"Okay if we tune in?" Montanez drawled.

In his office Raber sat behind the desk and switched on the overhead mike.

"What is your full name?" he began.

Goodone did not answer.

"You have the legal right to remain silent. Your age?"

No answer.

"You're thirty-seven," Raber said, and placed a color enlargement before Goodone. "Whose picture is that?"

Again, no answer.

"It's yours," Raber said, and glanced up at Orwell. "Major,

do you suppose this clam realized that during the past week the local police were looking over his shoulder?"

"No, captain. He sees no better than he fights. The evidence we have proves this clam helped drown Harry Shellenbach in a tub of water inside Lodge One. That means we charge him with first-degree murder."

"Mr. Goodone, do you want to comment?" Raber asked.

There was no answer.

"Major, would you explain the murder of Evelyn Noornan?"

"Certainly. Before eleven o'clock last Friday night, Miss Noornan left Lodge Twelve and tried to start a Corvette. She failed because Carl Krauthof had rendered the Corvette inoperative. Who appeared on the scene? This clam. Ah, what a ferocious fighter he was against an unarmed woman. This clam broke her jaw so she couldn't scream for help. She collapsed to the ground. This clam strangled her. We charge him with another first-degree murder."

"Mr. Goodone, do you want to make a comment?" Raber asked.

Goodone sat silent.

"Major, we know the water in Harry Shellenbach's lungs came from a tap in the bathtub inside Lodge One. We know Miss Noornan did not die in the crash of the Corvette on Route Seventeen where this clam piloted the club's Buick. Both murders were rigged to look like accidents. The police solved both murders. Mr. Goodone, may we hear from you?"

Sweat beaded Goodone's face, but he said nothing.

"Ah, he remains loyal to Gino Paladino," Orwell said pleasantly. "He clings to the criminal code—keep the lip buttoned. For five years this clam worked for Paladino. Paladino said smile and he smiled. Paladino said jump and he jumped. Paladino said drown Harry Shellenbach and he drowned Harry Shellenbach. Paladino said strangle Evelyn before she blabs to the police and he strangled Evelyn."

"Why is he so stupid?" Raber asked.

"Money prevents him from thinking."

"How much money, major?"

"In Paladino's two attaché cases we found over four

hundred fifty thousand dollars in cash. Also, there is the value of all that heroin packaged for street sale. Preliminary estimates say that is four million dollars. That's a lot of money."

"Yes, and the clam thought he was to share half of it. Major, he forgets about Paladino's plan for Monday night, September seventeenth."

"Yes. On Monday night the five employees were to fly in the helicopter to Paladino's farm on Long Island." Orwell laughed. "This clam was to kill Krauthof, Ramose, and Arragon and bury their bodies in the lonely woods. But Paladino is the brain. Only two of the gang are left. What was supposed to happen next?"

"A child knows that answer. Paladino kills this clam and walks out with all the loot. Mr. Goodone?"

"I was gonna kill—"

They waited.

Goodone's lips were set in a thin line, his eyes smoldering. Sweat stained his blue shirt and his hands were fists.

"Paladino had the brains," Raber offered. "We know he is a chemist and understood the use of poisons. What was to happen next?"

"On Tuesday night," Orwell answered, "in that lonely house on Long Island, Paladino and his clam sit at a table. The cash is spread before them and this clam can't keep his greedy eyes off it. Paladino proposes a toast to two smart men. He brings out a bottle of wine. He readies two glasses and there is a fast-acting poison in the bottom of this clam's glass. Paladino pours the wine and they drink. That poison hits the clam's stomach and—"

Goodone banged a fist on the desk. "I don't have to listen. I got rights. I'm leaving, okay?"

Raber said, "Officer Gladwyn," and she opened the door a moment later. "Return the prisoner," he added, and the two left.

"Let him stew, I think he'll crack," Orwell decided.

21

GINO PALADINO sat beside the desk in Raber's office. Raber switched on the overhead mike and leaned back.

"Mr. Paladino," he began, "this is not an interrogation. Consider it a conversation. Also, we are not being recorded. I thought that you might like to keep abreast of the developing situation as it affects you. Let me try a simple question. Where is the hyoid bone located?"

"I have no idea," Paladino answered politely.

"What is the hyoid?"

"I have no idea."

"The water in all the taps at Twin Springs is artesian supplied by the Borough of Fair Hills. What is that water's iron content?"

"I had no idea the water contained iron."

"What is that water's calcium content?"

"I have no idea."

"Did you know that water contained a chlorine additive?"

"No."

"Your ignorance amazes me." Raber smiled. "Artesian water is hard. Pond water is relatively soft and contains impurities such as bits of vegetable matter. Compare the two waters in a laboratory and they are readily distinguishable."

"If you say so, captain."

"At twelve thirty, on Saturday, September eighth, a lab test of the water found in Harry Shellenbach's lungs proved it to be artesian water and not pond water. Conclusion? He had been drowned, probably in a tub inside Lodge One and subsequently eased quietly into the adjacent pond. His death was not an accident, but a first-degree murder. Do you wish to make a comment?"

"Yes." Paladino shrugged gracefully. "The man had an enemy."

"Indeed he did, and the FBI reports that enemy had an IQ of 170. They further report that in your freshman year at CCNY you started premed and received an A in anatomy. Later, your major study was chemistry and pharmacology. As an A student in anatomy, you know the hyoid is a U-shaped bone at the base of the tongue. If that bone is fractured by strong fingers, the injury is lethal. Evelyn Noornan did not die from injuries suffered from the crash of a Corvette on Route Seventeen. A medical examiner for the New York State Police determined she died several hours before the crash from a fractured hyoid. That makes her death first-degree murder. Do you have any comment?"

"I certainly do, captain." Paladino smiled politely. "Miss Noornan was a very attractive woman."

"Yes, she was," Raber agreed. "But she had learned about your drug conspiracy at Twin Springs and intended to notify the police. She had to be murdered fast. As did Harry Shellenbach, for the same reason. You consider the local police stupid. Haven't they done a pretty good job?"

"I never called the local police stupid," Paladino murmured.

"It's Thursday night, nine o'clock, September thirteenth, on the screened porch of the farmhouse," Raber clipped off. "You and Paulo Goodone finished dinner, lit cigars, drank wine, and talked about the air freight business and drugs. I heard every word you said. I was ten feet from you. I gave specific evidence of your crime to the judge who issued that search warrant. I quote Goodone: 'How are things here?' I quote your answer: 'Peaceful, no trouble from the stupid local police.' By the way, do you always carry around a roll of nickels in your right pants pocket?"

"Captain, I have never carried such a roll."

"Let us shift to Lodge One, about ten o'clock, Friday night, September seventh. You stood with your back to the opened front windows with the light on in the main room. You faced Harry Shellenbach. In your left hand you held a bottle of Château Lafite-Rothschild. You told him it was a present and he reached for it. You brought your right hand out of your right pants pocket. Inside your fist was a roll of nickels. You clobbered him in the solar plexus and knocked him cold, correct?"

"You have a fertile imagination." Paladino smiled. "Do you supplement your low salary by writing mystery stories?"

"Your lawyers will learn more than I have told you before you face charges on two first-degree murders. Are you wearing a hairpiece?"

"No, it's a wig."

"After seven A.M., Saturday, September eighth, you told me Werner DeHaven found Shellenbach in the pond and he lived in Lodge Two?"

"Which 'he' do you mean?"

"Sorry, I garbled the grammatical reference. DeHaven lived in Lodge Two. You told me DeHaven was in Lodge Two with his wife?"

"Probably, that was the fact."

"The fact is you operated a call-girl racket. We subpoenaed toll-call records from Bell Telephone. Between April fifteenth and September sixth, scores of toll calls were made between Twin Springs and a Walter G. Prager in Newark. The call-girl business was brisk and you received a twenty percent commission, so Mr. Prager stated in a deposition. Frankly, at Twin Springs you were a babe lost in the woods. What did we know about you before the two murders? You knew nothing about how to operate a trout club. You had built a new room in the basement and had two locks on the door. You had trapped the front entrance on Haycock Road with a photoelectric eye and electrically charged the chain-link fence at night. You did not know how clearly ordinary conversation carries on a quiet night in the country, so Evelyn Noornan overheard about the drug racket. Belatedly you nailed shut those open Dutch doors on the unused stable. My God, you didn't even know that Harry Shellenbach was a private investigator with a powerful listening device to monitor conversation in the farmhouse!"

Slowly, Raber stood behind the desk.

"Who first uncovered your multimillion-dollar drug racket? A woman who bought women's accessories. Next, a second-rate private detective. Finally, a hick police force.

Gee whiz, Mr. Paladino, I'm trying to help you, see? We're the Keystone Kops. You just don't use the old bean."

Paladino rose. Raber took him by an elbow.

"I'll kinda steer you back to the big room, see?"

He led Paladino through headquarters, across a corridor, and into the civic center where he paused. Men and women worked at tables. A uniformed cowboy guarded a far door. A refreshment table was presided over by a young man sporting a chef's hat and jacket, a mustache, and dark glasses.

"Mr. Paladino," Raber murmured, "you are the cause of all this late activity. Do you remember Joe Arragon? He has an IQ of a hundred. You underestimated Joe. You planned to have Goodone murder him, but Joe planned to kill you on your Long Island farm. You see, you had strangled Evelyn Noornan. She was Joe's friend. Joe doesn't know about the hyoid bone. He didn't need to know, not with his strength. We move to the right, please."

They walked toward the headquarters table at the far side of the room where a gray-haired man sat between Major Orwell and a young man.

"Good evening, Mr. Davis," Raber said to the man in the middle. "I am returning this prisoner to your custody."

Paladino jerked loose from Raber.

"Don't you dare lay a hand on me again," he warned, and wheeled to Davis. "Enough of this nonsense. You illegally confiscated over four hundred fifty thousand dollars of my cash. I demand to be taken before a judge. I'll use part of that money for bail and immediate release."

"Said cash has been impounded," Davis advised. "Also, the IRS will determine if you paid income tax on it."

"Temporarily, I'll use other money for bail. I have two hundred thousand dollars in a business account in a Jersey City bank."

"Yesterday afternoon," Davis advised, "a United States attorney attached that money. It's unavailable."

There was an instant change in Paladino as he asked politely, "May I borrow a quarter to phone my attorney?"

"Lawrence Oppenheim," Davis explained, "has his own problems. For several months, we've been studying his connection to Empire Export and Import Company. He owns shares of its stock and has been funneling its funds overseas for the drugs. Mr. Oppenheim was arrested this afternoon and won't be able to make bail for himself until Monday."

Davis gestured to his right.

"Meet Major Orwell, head of Telford County's Investigative Staff."

Orwell stood and drew two documents from an inner jacket pocket. He used them to tap Paladino.

"Mr. Paladino," he said casually, "I'll end your problem of bail. I charge you with the first-degree murders of Evelyn Noornan and Harry Shellenbach. In New Jersey such charges are rarely bailable. I now give you your legal rights."

Orwell ticked off the particulars.

"Clear, Mr. Paladino?"

"Perfectly," Paladino acknowledged, and turned to Raber.

"Captain, it seems I underestimated your capabilities."

"No," Raber said politely, "you overestimated yours."

22

"Captain Raber, thank you for your cooperation," Mr. Davis said. "Two of our agents in the foreign branch will board a Pan Am plane at Shannon Airport. As soon as the three latest smugglers pass through Customs at International Airport in Philadelphia they'll be arrested and their luggage confiscated. That should complete the arrests in this drug conspiracy and the first news release will be made at eleven A.M. on Sunday."

"Very good, sir," Raber said, and began the amenities. "We needed your personal supervision tonight, your vast experience, and your department's superb manpower. Alone, our small department would have bungled the job." He bowed to Davis and turned to Orwell. "Thanks for your generous help and the full use of your men. You have always been most cooperative with the Fair Hills police."

Raber bowed to Orwell and returned to Davis.

"We have exhausted the sandwiches at our headquarters and will have some hungry men coming off duty shortly. Could that attendant at the refreshment stand deliver a fresh supply to us?"

"Certainly," Davis agreed, and nodded to the third man at the table.

Sam crossed to the table and talked to the attendant, who nodded. He picked up two plates of sandwiches and Sam started to return. The attendant started toward the Fair Hills police headquarters. A young woman stepped from the kitchens. In two swift movements she stripped off high-heeled shoes, carrying them as she trailed after the attendant.

A new man hurried in and whispered to Davis, who nodded. "Sam, bring Billingsley on the jump downstairs,"

Davis ordered. "Then issue orders to start evacuating." Davis whispered to Orwell, who nodded. They left.

Raber strode across the wide recreation center and entered the corridor where the young woman stood now wearing her shoes.

"Hi, Teresa," Raber said softly.

"Freddy, darling." She smiled. "It's been a great show."

"Yes, and it's about to end here."

"Please go in first, Freddy."

He entered with Teresa at his back. The attendant in the chef's hat loitered at the high desk. On desk duty, Lieutenant Waslewski talked to Montanez. The three policewomen and two local officers chattered and somebody said, "No, it's two murders."

"Don," Raber said loudly and tapped the attendant.

In the abrupt silence Don Lord of the local *Clarion* turned.

"Take off the disguise," Raber ordered.

Lord stripped off the mustache, the glasses, and chef's hat.

"Fred, it's the only way I could get inside. This is the biggest story I've ever handled and it's a scoop. I can just make wire service."

"Sorry, all news is to be held until eleven o'clock."

"Like hell it is!" Lord snapped. "I'm heading for a phone!"

"Will you cooperate or do you prefer arrest?" Teresa asked.

"Who the hell is she?" Lord demanded.

"She's Sergeant Musanti, County Investigative Staff," Raber said.

"By God, Fred, I'm the press! What's this arrest crap?"

"For forcing me to stand three hours in heels," Teresa said sweetly. "For penetrating a police guard on a sealed building. For violating security measures of the Treasury Department. And, for a poor disguise."

"How'd you tumble, damn it?"

"Mr. Lord, I'm particular about that word." She was amused. "You entered the building and Chief Hocking tipped us off."

"I'm phoning now," Lord insisted.

"Don," Raber said, "Sergeant Musanti has two medals for

valor. Or don't you keep up with the county news? She's a karate expert. She's a marksman, carries a Beretta, and—"

"Freddy, please," Teresa said. "You'll cooperate, Mr. Lord?"

"Is she really that good?" Scafide bubbled.

"She is really." Raber began to pile sandwiches on a paper plate. "How did you like her suit?"

"It's super!"

"She buys imports from Rome with a special pocket in the jackets for the Beretta. Grace, is there fresh coffee in the rear area?"

Officer Gladwyn nodded.

"That's a small-bore, short-barreled gun," Montanez drawled. "It's apt to be inaccurate. You said she's a marksman?"

Raber rounded the desk. "She compensates with the gun by firing in bursts." He waved a free hand. "Top job, everybody." He disappeared into the rear area.

More local officers crowded in. They ate, smoked, and talked. Ten minutes later, Chief Hocking entered and joined Waslewski.

"Where's the captain, Wally?"

"He wolfed sandwiches and coffee. I kept tabs on him in the rear area. He's asleep."

The chief raised his voice and said, "You did a great job tonight, everybody. We're closing shop. Hit the road. On Monday turn in chits for overtime. That's courtesy of the Treasury Department."

He entered the rear area where Raber slept in a tilted chair, his stockinged feet propped on a desk.

"There's one sure way," Hocking said softly, "to turn a clam into a singing canary."

Raber awakened and lowered his feet to the floor.

"Freddy, you show him proof he's been double-crossed. The luggage of the five employees was confiscated and exact lists compiled of the contents of their suitcases. I was interested only in that of Paladino. In his two attaché cases he carried the hefty sum of—brother, four hundred fifty-five thousand two hundred fifty dollars! In a suitcase he had several items I needed and Mr. Davis let me sign out for them. They had tried to interrogate Goodone, but he never opened his mouth. I went downstairs to where he was being held alone in the fire chief's office. I sent the two guards out. Hell, I figured if you could deck Goodone, I'd have no trouble."

"Right," Raber agreed.

"You know that plain little tin of aspirins I carry around?"

"Yes, but each is marked with a large A."

"Sure, but does Goodone know that? Everybody else asked him questions. I'd show him exhibits and—"

"You dally," Raber objected. "I admit, you—are—clever."

"Hah, listen to the twist! I showed Goodone items taken from Paladino's suitcases. I showed him a picture of a villa outside Lisbon. I told the clam Paladino purchased the villa in June. I showed him Paladino's passport. I showed him a one-way ticket to Lisbon on a TWA plane, date of departure September twenty-third. I gave him the final figure, four hundred fifty-five thousand two hundred fifty dollars, the cash in Paladino's two attaché cases. 'You thought you were to get half of that?' I asked him. 'Look at this, stupid.' I showed him a deposit slip for Empire's bank in Jersey City. It was filled out for a deposit of four hundred forty-eight thousand dollars. I pointed to the date, September nineteenth. I asked: 'Stupid, was Paladino going to pay you by check?' Last I showed him that plain tin of aspirin, each pill marked with a capital A. Arsenic for you, I told the clam. It was in Paladino's suitcase. Stupid, Paladino was going to kill you."

"Chief, you *know* arsenic is a slow-acting poison."

"So what?" Hocking countered. "If a clam can't tell aspirin from arsenic, he won't know arsenic acts slowly. So, the clam started to blab and I sent an SOS for Mr. Davis. Freddy, when I left them, the clam was singing like a canary. Names, dates, places, figures, Empire overseas, key personnel, and so on. How's that for the chief of the Hicksville police?"

"Very good."

Raber stood and stretched.

"One point, chief. When you return those items you

signed out for with Mr. Davis, what are you going to do with that deposit slip you filled out for four hundred forty-eight thousand dollars?"

Hocking snapped his fingers.

"Somehow it just happened to get lost."

They shook hands.

23

IN THE rear area at police headquarters in Fair Hills, Roy Boyce said, "Ho-hum, it's December thirtieth."

"You'd better scrounge us some new calendars," Fred Raber suggested.

"Will do. I bumped into John Barrington. He told me his wealthy guests who formed a corporation to buy the trout club take over the fifteenth of January. Did you know that Werner DeHaven is their president?"

Raber nodded.

"I expect him to hire Joe Arragon. Joe, we know, was a key witness in the conviction of Gino Paladino for two murders. The local prosecutor has no case against Joe and feels the feds may let him off with a parole. The same is true for Diego Ramose and his testimony for the state in the murder trial. Oh, that medicine Ramose was taking at Twin Springs was for hay fever. The other three men? Carl Krauthof will always be in trouble and drew a five-ten sentence for transportation of drugs. Paul Goodone has no worries for at least fifteen years. Gino Paladino? One life sentence for murder piled on top of another life sentence. Now where are we, Roy?"

"At the appointment of a female detective here," Boyce said. "Who gets it—Grace Gladwyn, Sande Nosse, or Rose Scafide?"

"You tell me," Raber countered as he sipped coffee.

"Not Grace, she's happy to be in the middle of the action at desk duty. Not Sande, she's too smart to let the odd hours of a detective interfere with the happy life of marriage. So it's Rose, before Major Orwell picks her off for his county staff. She wants to be another Teresa Musanti. Also, she's ambitious. She finished karate lessons. Montanez suggested she use a .22 automatic, and he's teaching her to become a marksman. She's hitting the books on criminal investigation and hands me new questions every day."

Boyce gave Raber his cherubic smile.

"Now that I've settled that question, when are you going to let me in on that letter you received from Evelyn Noornan's uncle?"

"Jeremiah French," Raber said. "It's two letters, Roy." He opened a letter. "In midwinter a fire started in Evelyn's home downstairs. Her father tossed her, aged three, from an upstairs window into a snowbank. The father tried to save the mother, but they both perished. Jeremiah French found the child and raised her."

Raber began to read:

> Greetings to Captain Raber and the Fair Hills Police Department for the new year. When I was in your town and met you, I subscribed to the county daily newspaper because I wanted to keep abreast of the murder cases. Many thanks for the conviction of Gino Paladino. Now I want you to know the truth about that helicopter pilot's story in court about something that he told happened in the bedroom of Lodge Twelve as he listened. I enclose Evelyn's last letter to me. Please read and return it.
>
> Sincerely,
> JEREMIAH FRENCH

Raber laid the letter aside and drew blue letter paper from an envelope, explaining "She wrote the time, six fifteen P.M., Friday, and she was murdered later that night." He began to read:

> Dearest uncle, I write this in haste. I have a cold and haven't been outside the lodge all day. Earlier a neighboring guest dropped in and asked if I needed anything at the drugstore as he was driving to town. I asked him to mail this letter, so it's a rush-rush job. I want you to be the first to learn

some wonderful news. I am breaking up the apartment arrangement with Adele Myrick in New York City. Uncle, I have met The Man! He is Harry Shellenbach, a guest in Lodge One. He is a simply terrible trout fisherman, but please forget that because we are in love! Harry and I are to be married soon and plan to live in his apartment in Caldwell, New Jersey. I'll keep my present job at Lord & Taylor's and commute to the city from Caldwell. Later, I'll write more fully and—OOPS, there's a knock at the door!

           Love,
           Eve

 Raber returned both letters to the envelope.
 "What a rotten shame!" Boyce said indignantly. "That greedy bastard Paladino really messed up their lives and—"
 Outside and overhead the fire alarm began to blast. Instantly, they rose and began to count. One-two, pause.
 "Southeast quarter," Boyce said as they hurried out.
 "A pulled alarm or phoned in?" Raber asked.
 "Phoned," Rose Scafide answered. "A kitchen fire, 218 Vernon. There's a paralyzed man upstairs."
 Raber and Boyce hit the stairway running.
 Chief Hocking strode from his office. "How bad is it?"
 "She was hysterical. I tapped the alarm and hit shortwave. Kelly is nearest."
 "Parisi?"
 "He's in Zone Four and rolling. Should I try to reach Kelly?"
 "No, it's touch and go. Keep out of it."
 Outside, a volunteer fireman arrived with a squeal of brakes. A heavy door rolled up. Another car slammed to a halt. A cool voice asked over the radio? "What's the pinpoint?"
 "Hurry, 218 Vernon," Scafide answered.
 "Will do, honey."

An engine roared into action. A siren began to wail. The first engine blasted off along Mercer Street. More cars arrived outside. A second engine sirened off, followed by a third.

"They'll never make it," Scafide said tensely.

"Keep the faith," Hocking said calmly. "It's Kelly all the way, or Parisi, or the captain and Roy. Maybe it's a volunteer fireman in the zone and he read the blasts. Rose, any one of 'em will wade in hell to get that cripple out."

The seconds ticked away.

A voice over shortwave: "Parisi here. You read me?"

"Yes," Scafide answered. "What about the paralyzed man?"

"No sweat, Kelly brought him out. The captain and Boyce have wrapped him in blankets and they're carrying him next door."

"What about the fire?"

"It's heating up. Wait a sec. . . . The first engine is coming in."

"Good work, sergeant."

"Hey, don't go uptight, honey. It's all in the day's work. Out."

"It sure is," Hocking said. "And it's all in the night's work, too. I am about to make a speech Officer Scafide."

"Yes, sir."

"When that fire horn blasts, everybody hops. We never know what it means till we get there. It's the same with police work. We never know if it's legwork or a complaint or a parking ticket or a rip job or some nut with a gun. It's overtime without pay, irregular duty hours, missing the family, and it can be in sleet or heat or rain. You learn to be fast and polite and cool and you don't push the power of that badge. That means you belong in the police.

"Officer Scafide, you're a youngster with a yum-yum figure. Before it's too late, turn in your resignation and get married. Being a cop—hell, have you any idea what the hell you're letting yourself in for?"

"I do."

"And you still want to be a cop?"
"Yes, sir."
"May God himself have mercy on you, officer."
A faint smile moved across Hocking's face.